A dangerous game

I clicked on the Web browser and started looking for a MUD to play.

"How about this one?" Kevin pointed at a heading on the list of MUDs scrolling across his computer screen: *http://www/sfp/furiousfour.*

I clicked to get to the home page. Then I read the text at the top of the page describing the game. *Archvillain Dirk Zorsan plans to take over the world with his arsenal of never-before-seen superweapons. No one can stop him except, perhaps, the Furious Four.*

I glanced at Kevin. "Sounds cool."

"Yeah!" Kevin agreed.

"We should definitely play at least one game," I said. I clicked my mouse. Kevin clicked his.

A heading filled the screen. We read, *Welcome to the world of "The Furious Four."* Then the words dissolved, and a man's face appeared. Half the face was hideously scarred, as though it had been burned in a terrible fire. The eyes gleamed with a strange reddish light.

The man looked so real, a shiver went down my spine. I stared at the screen, waiting for what would happen next. Suddenly, I heard a weird, raspy voice.

"I am Meltdown Man," the voice hissed. "Once left for dead by Dirk Zorsan in a chemical blast, I have now returned to get my revenge!"

CYBER ZONE™
Meltdown Man

CYBER ZONE™
Meltdown Man

S. F. Black

Troll

Copyright © 1997 by Troll Communications L.L.C.
and Creative Media Applications, Inc.

Published by Troll Communications L.L.C.

Art direction by Fabia Wargin.
Cover art by Broeck Steadman.

Printed in the United States of America.
10 9 8 7 6 5 4 3 2 1

CYBER ZONE™

ZONE

Meltdown Man

Chapter 1

Sports aren't my thing. I'm short and uncoordinated, and every time I try to play a sport there's a disaster. My gym teacher, Mr. Allen, can't stand me because I'm not athletic. But all the jocks, especially Corey Wilson and Ted Stern, love me. I'm the butt of all their jokes. And I hate them.

My friends and I are more into video games and computers. It's weird, but you can be totally uncoordinated in real life and still be cool in cyberspace. I'm one of the best game players in Centerburg Elementary. Ask anyone. I used to think that computers were the perfect way to escape from real-life problems, like gym class and bullies. Boy, was I wrong.

But I guess I'd better tell the story from the beginning.

"Let's see some hustle!" Mr. Allen bellowed.

It was a hot September afternoon. My gym teacher had dragged our whole gym class outside to play basketball. He'd said it would do us good to play out in the fresh air. But I didn't feel "good." I felt like I was melting in the hot sun. Plus, it was allergy season, and all that pollen made my eyes water and my nose itch.

"Kerchoo!" I sneezed loudly.

My best friend, Kevin Tyler, looked down at me sympathetically. He looked down because he's about a foot taller than I am. "Show some hustle!" he muttered sarcastically as the two of us ran forward to defend our basket.

Kevin and I were on the Blue team, as usual. Our pathetic squad was made up of the worst athletes in the whole school. And today we were playing against the Reds—the best athletes in the sixth grade.

It was the last two minutes of the game. The score was 42 to 14. We were getting crushed!

"Matt, look out!" shouted Carl Young, another Blue team nerd.

I turned quickly. Corey Wilson was trying to pass to Ted Stern, but his aim was off. The ball was heading straight for me.

I reached my hands out—and caught it! I just stood there for a moment, stunned. I had intercepted Corey Wilson's pass. It was a miracle! The only problem was that everyone on our team was waiting for me to take a shot.

"Hurry up, Matt—shoot the ball!" Chris Johnson yelled from across the court. Chris is the best basketball player in our group. He's pretty good at sports—so good I sometimes wonder why he doesn't hang around with the jocks. But I have a feeling it's because they don't want to hang around with him. Chris can be kind of obnoxious. I don't say that to Kevin, though. He likes Chris a lot.

I lifted the ball over my head, ready to take a shot. Ted Stern was moving in on me. In fact, he was looming over me like an eight-foot gorilla.

"You feel lucky, Shrimp?" he taunted.

"You bet, Godzilla," I retorted.

My adrenaline pumping, I leaped high into the air. Twirling around, I aimed the ball at the basket and let it go.

I blinked in the hot sunlight. Then I smiled. What a shot! The ball had traveled halfway down the court and landed right in the basket! Even though we were still going to lose the game, I had finally made a basket and it felt great. I pumped my fists into the air and started to cheer.

As I ran to celebrate with my teammates, I noticed something was wrong. My friends all had major scowls on their faces.

"You shot the ball into the wrong basket!" chirped a familiar voice. "I can't believe you're so lame!"

It was my sister, Crystal. Her class was having recess, and she was standing on the sidelines rolling her eyes at me. Crystal always follows me around—not because she admires me, but because she likes making fun of me every chance she gets. She's a major pest.

As I realized Crystal was telling the truth, my heart sank all the way to the tips of my sneakers. I couldn't believe it. For once I'd made a good shot, and look how it had turned out!

It was one of the worst moments of my life.

The time clock Mr. Allen had set on the sideline started to ring. I sneezed loudly. *Kerchoo!*

"Game over!" all the kids on the Red team hollered,

trading high-fives. "We creamed those losers!"

Kevin, Carl, and I looked at one another. Chris just frowned at us.

Mr. Allen blew his whistle and came over to me. "Don't feel too bad, Matt," he said. I squinted up at him, amazed that my gym teacher was actually being nice for a change. Then I saw the smirk on his face. "At least you shot the ball," he said. "Next time, just try to remember what side of the court your basket is on. Okay, Fumble-Fingers?"

Fumble-Fingers! I could feel anger boiling over inside me as the words echoed in my head. I really hated Mr. Allen. Teachers are supposed to be kind and encouraging, but he was just plain mean.

Mr. Allen blew loudly on his whistle. "Okay," he shouted. "Everyone get into the locker room and get changed."

As we walked toward the gym, the kids on the Red team all taunted me. "Way to go, Fumble-Fingers!" Ted Stern hooted.

"Matt, are you sure you don't need glasses?" quipped his buddy, Richie Martin.

"Hey, Shrimp, we really appreciate your helping us out like that," Corey Wilson shouted.

My cheeks started to burn. My friends and I had been losing badly enough. Why did I have to be the one to turn our loss into a total humiliation? For the millionth time, I started daydreaming about what it would be like if I could somehow be different. Like Superman or something. Klutzy, weakling Matt Harper by day, invincible superhero by night!

"Don't let Mr. Allen get to you," Carl muttered.

"I can't stand him," I growled. "In fact, I wish he would disappear off the face of the earth."

I don't think I really meant it. But I was mad, very mad. And you know what they say—be careful what you wish for, because you just might get it.

Chapter 2

I changed as fast as I could and went up to my locker to get my lunch. As I slammed the door shut, Kevin came up behind me.

"Hey, Matt," he said.

"Hey, Kevin," I replied glumly. "What's up?"

"After we eat lunch, do you want to play a few computer games?" Kevin suggested.

I smiled. "Sure, sounds excellent!"

Kevin has been my best friend since kindergarten. We both love computers and computer games, and we're both incredible klutzes. Another reason Kevin is my best friend is that he really knows how to cheer a person up. He knew that reminding me that our school computers had just been hooked up to the Internet was guaranteed to make me feel better about life.

In my opinion, the Net was the most exciting new thing that had ever happened at our school. I was on the Internet at home, too. For my birthday my parents had bought me a modem and a subscription to an on-line service. You wouldn't believe how hard I had to beg to get them to do it. But they had, and now I could go on-line anytime I wanted—or almost anytime. Mom wouldn't let me spend hours on the computer. She said spending too much time on-line was just like watching too much TV.

Kevin and I ran to the cafeteria, wolfed down our lunches, and headed upstairs to the tiny computer room. It looked more like a closet than a room. It didn't even have a window. But it did have four brand-new computers.

Kevin and I sat down side by side and logged on. On-line, Kevin calls himself *KevT.* I call myself *MHarp.* A lot of kids who go on-line give themselves fancy names like *Superstar* or *Wolfman,* but I think that's kind of stupid. Giving yourself a fancy name on-line won't really change who you are.

I clicked on the Web browser and started looking for a MUD to play. MUD stands for *Multiple User Dimension,* which is a mouthful even for a computer freak like me. But MUDs are the coolest on-line games. Lots of people around the world can play the same game at the same time. Plus, the story lines and graphics on MUDs are so well done that playing a good one is like going into a totally different world.

"How about this one?" Kevin pointed at a heading on the list of MUDs scrolling across his computer screen: *http://www/sfp/furiousfour.*

"Furious Four?" I murmured. "That's a new one. Let's see what it is."

Kevin clicked on the heading with his mouse. His screen instantly showed the home page. That's the page that introduces a game. It tells you when a MUD was put on the Net and who programmed it, and what the MUD is about.

I clicked to get to the home page myself and peered at the copyright at the bottom. "The game was programmed by some company called Split-Face Productions," I read out loud. "I've never heard of them."

Then I read the text at the top of the home page describing the game. *Archvillain Dirk Zorsan plans to take over the world with his arsenal of never-before-seen superweapons. No one can stop him except, perhaps, the Furious Four.*

I glanced at Kevin. He was reading the description, too. "Sounds cool," I said. "Do you want to try it?"

"Yeah!" Kevin agreed. He squinted at the screen. "Hey, that's wild!"

"What's wild?"

"Check out where Split-Face Productions is from!"

I stared down at the copyright again. *Split-Face Productions, Greenvale, New York.*

"Wow!" I said.

Greenvale, New York, is where Kevin and I live. It's a fairly small town. I guess it's nice and all, but it's dull. Our main street is called Main Street, and we don't have a mall. That's why it was so surprising that Split-Face Productions was in our town. Greenvale isn't exactly crawling with high-tech computer and software companies.

"Are you ready to play?" I said.

"Definitely," Kevin replied.

I clicked my mouse. Kevin clicked his.

A heading filled the screen. We read, *Welcome to the world of "The Furious Four."* Then the words dissolved, and a man's face appeared. Half the face was hideously scarred, as though it had been burned in a terrible fire. The eyes gleamed with a strange reddish light.

The man looked so real, a shiver went down my spine.

"Cool," Kevin said under his breath.

The graphics in this MUD were the most awesome ones I'd ever seen. I stared at the screen, waiting to see what would happen next. Usually some text appears explaining what the game is all about and how to play. But no text appeared. Instead, I suddenly heard a weird, raspy voice.

"I am Meltdown Man," the voice hissed. "Once left for dead by Dirk Zorsan in a chemical blast, I have now returned to get my revenge!"

Chapter 3

I almost jumped out of my skin. There are computers that have voice capacity. Most video games do—or at least they have some kind of sound track. But I knew our school computers didn't. Our computer teacher, Mr. Cochran, was always complaining about how our school system was so cheap that our computers had no voice capacity whatsoever. I turned to Kevin. He looked as scared as I felt.

"What was that?" I gasped.

"I don't know," Kevin whispered. "It can't be the computer."

"But it sounded like the computer!"

We stared wide-eyed at our terminals. Text describing the characters and the rules of the game was scrolling across both our screens now, but we were too scared to read it.

"It was Meltdown Man," I hissed. "He talked!"

"But that's impossible!"

Just then I saw a shadow move behind the movie screen that was set up in the corner of the room.

I froze, goose bumps rising on my arms. Something was back there.

Then I heard laughter. I looked up to see Chris Johnson poking his head out from behind the screen.

"You should have seen your faces!" he chortled. "You two looked like you were about to lose it!"

I gaped at Chris in disbelief. "That voice was you?" I said coldly. I didn't want Chris to know how badly he'd scared me. "What are you doing here? How did you even know we were going to be here?"

"I told him to meet us," Kevin said softly. "I thought we could all play together."

"Oh," I grunted.

"That was a pretty good trick, Chris," Kevin said. "But how did you know we'd be playing this game?"

"Because it's the coolest new MUD there is," Chris replied. "I just discovered it last night. It's totally awesome."

He plopped down in front of the computer next to me and switched it on. "Let me just log on, and I'll totally whip you guys."

"Great," Kevin said.

I didn't say anything. Chris was busy typing in his on-line name, *SuperCris*. I grimaced to myself. It figured Chris would name himself something like that.

On my computer screen, Meltdown Man's face was fading from view now, but his eyes still shone bright red from the screen. It was as if he were watching me. Another shiver went up my spine. Then his eyes vanished, too.

Do you want to play? The words appeared on the screen. I clicked on *yes*. The game instructions scrolled across my screen. I leaned forward to read them. Kevin did, too.

"Let me know when you're ready," Chris drawled. He was leaning back in his chair, making it extra obvious that he'd already played the game and didn't even need to read over the instructions.

Every player must pick a character, I read silently. *The four characters are Meltdown Man, Steelsides, Rubber Band Man, and Ice Fingers.* I quickly read to the end of the instructions.

"You guys done yet?" Chris asked impatiently. "I want to play. Only I get to be Meltdown Man."

I shook my head. "No way," I said firmly. "*I* get to be Meltdown Man, or I'm not playing."

Chris glared at me. I glared back. I wasn't going to back down. Chris didn't look like he was, either.

"Come on, Chris," Kevin said. "Let Matt be Meltdown Man. You already played the game, right? So you already got to be Meltdown Man. Give Matt a chance."

Chris pushed out his bottom lip. "Okay," he said grumpily. "I'll be Steelsides, I guess."

"Cool." Kevin smiled. "I'll be Ice Fingers."

We typed our names in and started playing.

Chris hadn't been kidding when he'd said that this was a totally awesome game. Meltdown Man was the leader of a band of superheroes. Rubber Band Man could stretch his limbs out as far as he wanted or shrink them to miniature size. Ice Fingers could freeze his enemies with a touch of his frosty fingertips. Steelsides had a steel-hard skin that could deflect any knife or bullet. All four had come to Dirk Zorsan's fortress to try to steal his secret formula. This evil villain planned to take over the world with his deadly weapon.

Dirk Zorsan was really scary. He was dressed head to toe in a scaly black suit. He even wore a black mask over his face, and his gloved fingers were tipped with sharp, spearlike razors.

The goal of the game was to get into Dirk Zorsan's laboratory and steal his secret formula. It sounded simple, but it wasn't. Dirk Zorsan had an army of robot henchmen to protect him. His steel fortress was protected by vipers, crocodiles, fierce baboons, and a zillion mines and booby traps. Only the very best players would make it to the fortress. Once inside, there were more terrifying opponents to beat.

All the characters hated Dirk Zorsan, but Meltdown Man hated him the most. It was thanks to Dirk Zorsan that half his face was burned off. Years before, when Meltdown Man was a brilliant young scientist, Dirk Zorsan had tried to kill him by blowing up his laboratory. Meltdown Man had lived, but his face was scarred and his eyes were injured in the explosion. Now, when Meltdown Man got angry, his eyes turned into lethal laser beams. He could melt down anything just by looking at it.

All the characters were cool, but Meltdown Man was the coolest. I sucked my breath in as the game began for real.

"Weird," Kevin murmured beside me as we played.

"Weird how?" I asked, amazed at how realistic the game's graphics were.

"Why does Meltdown Man have to get mad before he can use his laser vision? I mean, how can you tell if he's getting mad or not?"

"Kevin, you're being too scientific about this,"

Chris answered. "He doesn't really have to get mad. Heck, he's not even real. You just punch in the right power code from the list at the start of the game."

"So how do you use the codes during the game? The list isn't on the screen while you play." Kevin's voice was puzzled.

"You have to memorize them," Chris told him in a superior voice.

I clicked my mouse, sending Meltdown Man racing across the field of land mines that led to the moat around Dirk Zorsan's steel fortress. My fingers sped over the keys. From all directions Zorsan's baboons came leaping out at me. Seconds later, crocodiles climbed out of the moat toward me. Playing *The Furious Four* was an incredible experience. It was about ten times as fast-paced as any other computer game I'd ever played. You couldn't lose your concentration even for a second, or you were dead. I couldn't remember ever playing so hard.

Kevin and Chris were playing hard, too. I could hear their fingers tapping over their keyboards as they tried to keep up with me. But it was no use. I was getting closer and closer to Dirk Zorsan's stronghold and leaving my friends far behind.

"Hey, Matt," Kevin said as I battled Dirk Zorsan's robot henchmen to storm the door of his metal fortress. "Have you played this before or something?"

"No way. I never even heard of it until today."

"Well, it sure looks like you've played it before," Chris said sulkily. I knew why he wasn't happy. Whatever game we play, Chris likes to cream me. But not today.

"I guess I just found a game I like," I murmured smugly. Chris cringed as Steelsides was pulled underwater by a giant crocodile. His steel skin made him sink like a stone. He was finished. A second later, Ice Fingers was consumed in a rolling ball of fire.

My friends were out of the game, but I wasn't. I punched in a code, and Meltdown Man's eyes lit with a furious red glow. I shuddered. I knew it was just a computer image, but it looked so real—almost as though Meltdown Man were in the room with us. I focused his laser gaze on the steel door of Dirk Zorsan's fortress. The door burst into white-hot flames.

Then I heard something that almost made me jump out of my seat. It was a loud ringing.

"It's the fire alarm!" Kevin exclaimed.

"I didn't know we were having a fire drill today," Chris said.

"Me, either!" I burst out.

We all looked at one another. "Maybe it's a real fire!" Kevin breathed.

Chapter 4

We leaped up and ran for the door. We didn't even take the time to turn off our computers. Out in the hall, it was total chaos. Kids were milling around everywhere as teachers frantically tried to direct them to the fire exits.

"It's probably nothing," Chris remarked as he stepped into the hallway.

"Still, I guess we'd better go outside, just in case," Kevin said nervously.

I agreed. I definitely didn't want to get caught in a real fire. I followed Chris and Kevin down the hall, but so many kids were piling out of classrooms all around that I soon lost my friends in the crowd.

"Kevin, Chris, wait up!" I called out, trying to see over the sea of kids. Unfortunately, when you're short, like me, that's not always easy.

"They went that way," said a voice behind me. I spun around. A kid was standing there, pointing down the hall. He looked about my age, but he was even shorter and thinner than I am. He had dark brown hair and looked like a regular kid except for one thing. He was wearing dark sunglasses.

He must think they make him look cool, I thought. I felt almost sorry for him—the sunglasses were really big and dark, and they didn't make him look cool at all. In fact, he looked awful.

I had a nagging feeling that I'd seen this kid somewhere before. Maybe I'd recognize him if he took his shades off.

"How do you know who I'm looking for?" I said.

The kid smiled. "I saw you guys coming out of the computer room together," he answered.

"Oh." I trudged forward. Mr. Allen was standing at the exit at the end of the hall. He had a bullhorn and was ordering everyone to line up and go outside "in an orderly fashion."

"Don't panic," he hollered at the crowd. "We have no reason to believe this is a real fire, but, to be safe, we're all going outside until the custodians can track down the source of the problem."

"So what were you guys doing in the computer room?" the kid asked eagerly.

I shrugged. Why was this weird kid being so friendly? "Just playing games," I said.

The boy suddenly leaned his face toward mine. "*The Furious Four?*" he whispered.

"Yeah, why?"

His voice became lower and more urgent. "Don't play that game!" he pleaded. "Stop while there's still time."

I stared at him. I wanted to say, "Are you crazy?" but that would have been a pretty rude thing to say to some kid I didn't even know. "Hey, it's just a game," I said instead.

The kid didn't say anything.

Just then I heard someone call my name. "Matt! Matt, over here!" I peered down the hall and saw Kevin and Chris. They were trapped against a row of lockers by a bunch of second-graders. I waved and grinned. Then I looked back to where that strange kid had been standing. But he was gone.

Chapter 5

"**D**on't hog the phone line for hours, Matt," Mom said.

I didn't say anything. I just hunched down over my desk and flicked the switch on my computer. The screen lit up. So did the light on the modem beside the phone. Mom and Dad had promised me that soon they'd get me my own phone line for my modem, but they hadn't done it yet. That was why Mom didn't want me to stay on-line for long. She claimed computer nuts like me were worse than teenage girls when it came to hanging out on the phone.

"It's not the same," I told her. "I mean, girls just yak. But I surf the Web, find out stuff, visit the chat rooms, play games, and do cool stuff like that."

"So you talk and play games," Mom said. "That doesn't sound all that different to me."

I tried to explain how it was different. But Mom didn't get it. She's not big on anything that involves technology. Sometimes I think she wouldn't drive a car if she didn't have to.

"Matt, are you listening? You can stay on that machine

for an hour and no more," Mom called up the stairs.

"An hour and a half," I shouted back. When it comes to dealing with parents, you have to know how to bargain.

"Okay, an hour and a half," Mom replied.

I smiled. My mom is actually pretty cool. I didn't think it would take me more than an hour and a half to play a quick game or two of *The Furious Four*—so long as Kevin was there, like he'd said he would be. While we were standing outside waiting for the fire alarm system to get fixed, we'd agreed to play that night.

The school janitor had said later that the alarm system had suddenly gone nuts for no reason. Ten minutes after the fire alarm had started ringing, it mysteriously stopped. By then the fire department had arrived. They'd checked the building and the wiring, but they couldn't find anything wrong.

Everyone had talked about it for the rest of the day. But I didn't say much. I kept remembering how I had made Meltdown Man set fire to the door of Dirk Zorsan's fortress just when the alarm started ringing.

Only a coincidence, right?

I frowned. Talking to that strange kid in the hall had scared me a little, but now I was pretty sure I knew what was behind his mysterious warning. He was jealous because my friends and I had discovered the coolest new game on the Net, and now we were going to be playing it a lot.

In fact, I couldn't wait to play it again. I just hoped Kevin was ready, too. There was only one way to find out—check my E-mail.

I hastily typed in *MHarp* to log on and then went to my mailbox.

I grinned as a message flashed up on the screen: *Mail is waiting.* I clicked on the screen with my mouse, and a ribbon of letters instantly appeared. *Hey, you're late—K.* My grin widened. It was Kevin.

I pulled down a new window to send him a message. *Sorry,* I typed, *I had a little Mom trouble.*

How long did she give you? A window appeared with Kevin's return message.

An hour and a half.

All right, Kevin wrote. *Let's go.*

I pushed my mouse and started clicking. I was hoping we could play *The Furious Four* without waiting. At night, sometimes, the Net gets really crowded and you don't get to play the game you want. But today Kevin and I were in luck, because no one but us was waiting to play *The Furious Four.*

I didn't get it—a cool new game like that, and no one in the whole world wanted to play it but me and my best friend? Still, I wasn't going to argue.

I clicked the mouse to get into the game.

Ready, Kev? I asked.

Affirmative, he typed back.

Cool, I wrote. *I get to be Meltdown Man.*

Again? Kevin replied.

Sure, I typed. *Why not?*

Fine with me, I guess, Kevin answered.

Then another window appeared on the screen. *Hey,* it read. *You guys aren't seriously going to play without me, are you?—SuperCris.*

I groaned aloud. "I might have known Chris

Johnson would show up," I said to myself grumpily.

Hey, dude. Awesome. We'll play three-way, Kevin wrote.

All right! But I get to be Meltdown Man! Chris declared.

I sighed. I knew it was only fair that Chris get to be Meltdown Man this time. But I didn't feel like being fair. I wanted to be Meltdown Man again.

I hesitated. Then my fingers flashed over the keyboard. *Let's duel for it,* I wrote. *Let me be Meltdown Man the first round. You can be any of the others. Winner takes all.*

What does that mean? Kevin demanded.

If Chris gets a higher score than I do, I typed back, *he gets to be Meltdown Man for the next month. If I get a higher score, I do.*

A smiley face appeared on the screen. It looked like this, :-), and Chris had typed the words *You're challenging me? SuperCris?* next to it.

Yup, I replied. I wanted to beat Chris so badly that my fingertips were tingling.

Okay, Chris wrote. *You're on, dude.*

We clicked to start the game. Faster than you would believe, we were sucked into the world of *The Furious Four.*

Meltdown Man raced across the screen. His first job was to make it to the moat around Dirk Zorsan's fortress. Guns were firing from all directions. I sent him rolling and dodging between the bullets. There were also land mines to worry about. I moved Meltdown forward when, suddenly, an explosion filled the screen.

For a moment, I thought Meltdown Man had been

creamed, but then I breathed a sigh of relief. It had been a near miss, but Meltdown was safe. Still, worse danger was to come. Meltdown Man had to battle Dirk Zorsan's crocodiles. He would need all the help I could give him.

My heart thudding, I pressed a power code for Meltdown Man. The code was the letters *XTY*. For a moment, I was surprised I knew that. I had only played the game once, and I hadn't bothered to reread the codes before we started this time. I'd figured it would take me a lot longer than one game to memorize all the power codes. Instead, it was like I just knew what I had to do. Now the weapons on Meltdown Man's belt were operational. *Zip!* I zapped three of Dirk Zorsan's flesh-eating crocodiles with a stun gun. Then I leaped across the moat and swung through an unguarded window into Zorsan's terrible fortress.

Meltdown Man moved down a dark hall—and ran straight into Dirk Zorsan! There was no time to run. He had to fight. I pressed the *Up* key and leaped at Meltdown's worst enemy.

The graphics in this game were unbelievable. It was almost like virtual reality without the headset. Every time Meltdown Man jabbed at Dirk Zorsan, I thought I could feel the blows pummeling my own body. *Bam! Pow! Crunch!*

I smiled to myself as I glanced at Chris's character, Steelsides, battling Dirk Zorsan's robot henchmen far behind me. Chris was fighting hard, but there was no way he was going to beat me in this game. My fingers sped over the keyboard. I pushed the mouse across the desktop, hitting the codes I needed to give Meltdown Man his full range of powers.

The power code for meltdown vision danced into my mind: *XZMLT.* On the screen, Meltdown Man's eyes lit with a red glow. Then, as I pressed the control buttons, Meltdown Man turned his terrifying gaze on Dirk Zorsan.

Zorsan was fighting with everything he had. So were his robots. Steelsides had already taken a number of hits. A blue light appeared around his body. That meant that Steelsides's magic steel shield was weakening.

Chris must really be sweating, I thought happily. I could just imagine him leaning over his keyboard, punching the keys so hard his whole desk shook. But it was no good. Dirk Zorsan's robots were beating him. Meltdown Man was beating him. I was beating him! I laughed aloud as, on the screen, Dirk Zorsan's robots moved in on Steelsides. He vanished in a puff of smoke. Chris had done his best, but he was no match for Zorsan—or me.

I fixed Dirk Zorsan in Meltdown's deadly gaze. The black-clad villain ducked out of the way. I pressed my advantage and raced toward the secret formula. That was where I made my mistake. I didn't know the laboratory was booby trapped. The screen turned blood red as Meltdown Man was swallowed up in a blaze of fire.

Good job, Meltdown, the screen flashed. *Better luck next time.* Then the winning player appeared on the screen. I had beaten Chris. Kevin had played Ice Fingers during the game, but he hadn't even made it past Dirk Zorsan's moat. I sighed in satisfaction as the question *Do you want to play again?* flashed in bold letters across the screen.

Hey, SuperCris. Play again :-)? I typed in. *Or have you had enough?*

Chris didn't answer. A message flashed up saying that player three was quitting the game.

The words *Game Over* filled the screen.

Hey, Kevin wrote. *I don't believe it, Matt. You won.* He put in a grin face. *Have you been practicing?* he added. *You've only played this game twice in your whole life!*

No, I typed back. *I guess I'm just getting better at computer games, that's all—right, SuperCris?*

Chris didn't answer. I almost thought he'd signed off. But then a message from him appeared on the screen. *Anyone can win if they know all the power codes, MHarp. If you haven't been practicing, how did you learn them all? I thought you never played this game before today. I guess you lied.*

I did not lie! I typed. *I guess I'm just a fast learner.*

Or you played it before, Chris wrote back. He added a flame sign to let me know that he was really mad. That's what people do when they're getting ready to fight someone over the Net.

I gulped. I hadn't meant to get on Chris Johnson's bad side. I took a breath. *Look,* I typed. *Are you trying to say you don't think I won fair and square?*

You won, Chris wrote after a minute. *You can be Meltdown Man.* Then he added, *I don't want to be him, anyway. He gives me the creeps.*

Suddenly I remembered the warning the weird kid at school had given me. I looked at the screen. Meltdown Man's face was staring out at me. He didn't look as grotesque to me as he had the first time I played the game, though. In fact, he looked almost friendly. His mouth curved up at the corners as though he were smiling at me.

As if we were partners.

He doesn't give me the creeps, I typed. *I think he's the coolest!*

Chris didn't answer.

Me, too, Kevin agreed. *Hey, Matt, will you show me what codes are best to use to get by different bad guys and traps?*

Sure, why not? I answered, feeling proud of myself.

"Matt, your hour and a half is up. Get off the phone. Now." It was my mom.

Sorry, guys, I have to go, I typed quickly. *Thanks for the game.*

Chris still didn't say anything.

Bye, Kevin wrote. *Let's play again soon so you can show me those codes.*

You bet, I wrote. I logged off and flipped the power switch on my computer. Then I wrinkled up my forehead, confused. While I'd been playing the game, somehow I'd just known which keys to press to unleash Meltdown Man's powers. But now, no matter how hard I tried, I couldn't remember any of them.

Chapter 6

Chris was still mad at me the next morning. When he, Kevin, and I met up on the school steps just before the first bell, Chris said, "So, Matt, I guess you think you're pretty smart."

I wasn't sure what he meant. "Huh?"

"I'm talking about the way you said you hadn't played *The Furious Four* that much," Chris declared. "No way you could have memorized all those power codes in one day. It's cool. I don't mind if a guy uses a few tricks to win. I just want you to know I'm on to your game."

He smirked at me. "I'll tell you what. So long as we both agree the bet we made is off, I'm willing to forget you cheated last night."

Cheated? I stared at him in disbelief. Why couldn't Chris just accept that I had won fair and square? "No way," I retorted. "We made a deal, remember?"

I looked at Kevin for support, but Kevin was staring down at his sneakers. I could tell he deliberately wasn't looking in my direction. That made me feel weird.

"I did not cheat," I proclaimed hotly.

Just then the bell rang. We were immediately surrounded by a ton of kids pushing their way up the steps. Chris disappeared in the crowd. Kevin and I slowly walked through the double doors.

When I got to my locker, I turned to Kevin. "Can you believe what a sore loser Chris is?" I said. "Why can't he just accept that I beat him?"

Kevin sighed. "Well, it was kind of strange how great you did," he mumbled.

I was shocked. I couldn't believe my own best friend wasn't on my side. "So you think I'm a cheat, too, huh?" I said huffily.

Kevin shifted from one foot to the other. "I didn't say that, Matt! I just don't understand how you memorized all the power codes so fast. I mean, you're good at computer games, but it always takes you forever to learn stuff."

I bit my lip. Kevin was right. I wasn't usually very good at remembering numbers. It had taken me weeks to learn the power codes for *Firebomb,* the last MUD we'd played.

Then I shrugged. "Maybe I'm just getting better," I said coldly. "I don't understand why you and Chris are getting so worked up. Maybe you don't like losing."

"Matt, that's not true," Kevin protested. "It's just that you're so intense about this game."

"What are you talking about?"

"Why do you have to be Meltdown Man every time we play? It's not like you to be so pushy."

"Yeah, well, I bet you'd never get mad at Chris for being too pushy," I murmured.

Kevin sighed. "No, but Chris is different."

"Maybe I want to be different, too," I shot back.

"It's okay to be different, but you don't have to be so selfish," Kevin said.

36

"What do you mean?"

"Well, maybe I want to be Meltdown Man, too," Kevin replied. "It's not fair for you to take the best character every single time we play the game. Like that bet you made with Chris—you didn't even bother to ask me how I felt about it."

I suddenly felt bad. Kevin had a point. "Fine," I said stiffly. "If that's what's bugging you, you be Meltdown Man next time we play. I don't care."

Kevin grinned. "Cool," he said, clapping me on the back. "Let's go, or we'll be late for class."

That morning we had computer with Mr. Cochran. He's a really terrific teacher. He even gets kids who hate computers interested in working with them. I sometimes wish my mom had had a teacher like Mr. Cochran when she was a kid. Maybe then she wouldn't think computers were so boring and awful.

That day Mr. Cochran was explaining different computer languages. They work by translating English (or any other human language) into numbers so different computers can "speak" to each other. Numbers are the only things computers can understand.

It was all pretty fascinating—at least to me. But even though computer is my favorite class and Mr. Cochran is my favorite teacher, I soon almost wished I were somewhere else—anywhere else—even gym, maybe. Because the moment I walked into class, Chris started bugging me.

"So, Harper, is the bet off?" he asked as I walked in.

"No," I answered.

Kevin looked at me in surprise. "But I thought you said you didn't care who was Meltdown Man," he said.

"Well, I do. I mean, I like being Meltdown Man," I said defensively. "Anyway, I won my bet with Chris."

Chris and I locked eyes for a moment. Then he shook his head. "I don't believe you," he muttered.

I glanced back over at Kevin. He looked the other way.

None of us said anything the rest of class, which was very unusual. See, Mr. Cochran lets kids talk in class. He says having dialogue is a great way to learn. I think he's right. But today my friends were giving me the silent treatment.

By the time the class was almost over, I'd had enough.

I turned to Chris. "Okay," I said, "the bet's off."

He smiled like a cat who'd just swallowed a thousand-pound canary. "Excellent," he said eagerly. "So you guys want to get together at lunch for a quick game?"

"Sure!" Kevin said. I could tell he was glad the fight was over. "What do you say, Matt?"

I shrugged. I knew I should just say *sure,* too, but I didn't feel like it. "I don't know," I mumbled. "I have some research I have to do at the library."

"Matt, come on, it'll be fun," Kevin pleaded.

"No, I'm not in the mood," I replied. "You guys play."

When the lunch bell rang, I walked to the library by myself. It was silent as a tomb in there. In our school, the library isn't exactly the most popular place to spend your lunch hour. I read an old Mystery Mutant comic book, then glanced over some computer textbooks. But my heart wasn't in it. By the time lunch was half over, I was wishing I had agreed to play *The Furious Four* with my friends.

After all, it didn't matter that much whether I got to be Meltdown Man or not. Did it?

Finally, I slung my backpack over my shoulder and headed upstairs to the computer room. The door was open. "Hey, Kevin. Hey, Chris," I called as I walked in.

But there was no one there.

My fingertips started to tingle. *They must have decided not to play after all,* I thought. I felt strangely glad. Now I'd get to play, and I'd definitely get to be Meltdown Man!

I quickly logged on.

In moments an ominous-looking silhouette of Dirk Zorsan's fortress appeared on the screen. The blood-colored words *Welcome to the world of "The Furious Four"* were below.

"All right!" I murmured.

Then I heard the door click shut behind me. "Gotcha!" said a voice.

I whirled around to see Chris standing there. "Hi, Chris," I stammered. "Where's Kevin?"

"He's outside with Carl and Mark," Chris answered. "He didn't want to play without you," he added meaningfully. "He said it wouldn't be any fun."

"Oh," I said guiltily. "Well, I came here looking for you guys, but since you weren't here, I figured I'd play alone."

Chris smiled. "Only now you don't have to play alone," he said softly. "Because I'm here. What do you say we have a rematch? One game, winner takes all."

"You mean the winner gets to be Meltdown Man for a month?"

"No. Forever."

I looked at Chris. There was a strange, intense expression in his eyes. "I don't know," I fumbled.

"Are you chicken?" Chris demanded.

"No, I—" But my voice was drowned out by the bell. In a way I was relieved. I didn't really want to play a challenge game with Chris for the lifelong rights to Meltdown Man. But in another way I was disappointed. I wanted to show Chris Johnson that I was the only person who could truly be Meltdown Man. Me and no one else!

"What a bummer." Chris scowled. "I can't believe lunch is over already!"

"Me, either," I agreed. "I guess we'll have to play another time, huh?"

I scooped up my backpack, and we went out into the hall. Suddenly, I spotted the kid—that kid who'd given me the mysterious warning.

My heart started thumping. "Sorry, I've got to go," I told Chris. "There's someone I have to talk to."

I sprinted down the hall. The kid was just ahead of me, but no matter how fast I went, I couldn't quite catch up with him. "Wait up!" I called, out of breath.

He stopped and turned around. He looked even more bizarre this time than he had before. For one thing, he was as pale as a ghost. For another, he was wearing different sunglasses—a bigger and darker pair.

What a weirdo! I thought.

I finally managed to catch up with him. "I just wanted to ask you a question—" I started. But before I could finish, the kid shook his head.

Then he said something. Although I was standing next to him, his voice was far away. I couldn't hear clearly what he said, but it sounded like "Too late!"

Then he spun on his heel and turned the corner. For a brief moment I just stood there, too stunned to say anything. When I realized the kid was leaving, I ran to catch up with him. But when I looked around, he was gone. The hall was empty.

I blinked. It was like he had vaporized, just vanished into thin air. "What a weirdo," I repeated aloud. But my insides were knotting up. Who was this kid anyway? And what did he mean by "too late"?

Chapter 7

I was still thinking about the weird kid when school ended that afternoon. *I'm sure I've seen him around before,* I thought as I opened my locker.

I jumped as someone tapped me on the shoulder. Then I took a deep breath. It was only Kevin. "Hey!"

Kevin smiled. "Hi, Matt. Do you want to come over to my house this afternoon?"

"Sure," I said with a grin. I'd been a little worried that Kevin might still be mad at me about wanting to be Meltdown Man all the time. But now I could see he wasn't. "Let's go."

We left the building and strolled toward Kevin's house.

Kevin lives three blocks from school and only a block from me. I think a big reason we're such good friends is because we're practically neighbors. At Kevin's house I called my mom to tell her where I was. "We're going to hang out here for the rest of the afternoon," I said. "Well, we might go to the park . . ."

"Okay," Mom said. "But be home before dark. Or else!"

I made a face. It gets dark pretty early in late September. "But Mom—"

"No *buts,* Matt Harper," Mom cut in. "Remember that poor boy who disappeared a couple of days ago? Promise me that as soon as it starts getting dark, you'll head straight home."

Mom had been extra paranoid the past few days because this kid from our town had disappeared. I didn't know much about it—just that some kid in the sixth grade at Tolland Middle School, the school on the other side of town, hadn't come home one afternoon. The police had looked for him everywhere, but they hadn't found him. There were posters with his picture up all over town. The kid's parents were offering a reward to anyone who helped find him.

I had to admit it was pretty creepy, but I still thought Mom was overreacting. I'd been going over to Kevin's house every other afternoon for the last five years. And Kevin and I were always together. What could happen?

Still, I knew better than to try and say that to Mom. She's the world-champion worrier.

"Okay. I promise."

"Good. See you tonight. And remember, *before dark or else.*"

"Or else," I repeated. I said good-bye, hung up, and rolled my eyes at Kevin.

"My mom is such a worrywart," I said. He smiled knowingly. His mom is the same way.

Kevin and I had a great time. First we made hot fudge sauce in the microwave and ate it over bubble-gum ice cream. After that, I suggested we go on-line for a while. But Kevin shook his head. "Nah, I don't feel like it," he said. "Let's go to the pond instead. I've got this new boat I want to try out."

Kevin and his dad are really into sailing. But there aren't any places to go sailing around Greenvale. So they make model boats and sail them on the pond. My dad says that's because Kevin and his family are eccentric. *Eccentric* is a fancy word for "wacky." I guess it is kind of wacky, but Kevin is really into it. He makes great model boats, too.

"Sure," I agreed. "Let's see her."

I said *her* because Kevin told me real sailors always talk about their boats as if they were girls. Don't ask me why. It's just some strange sailor thing, I guess.

Kevin grinned and brought out a big cardboard box. A blue-and-white sailboat was inside it. It was such a perfect model, even I was impressed.

"Wow," I said. "That's the best one you ever made!"

"Yeah," Kevin said proudly. "She sails pretty well, too."

He tucked the box under his arm, and we started toward the park. It was a perfect day to go to the pond. The sky was blue and clear. The leaves on the trees were already changing color, but it was still warm enough that I could wear just a light jacket. The pond looked peaceful and beautiful.

Kevin carefully put the boat into the water. He kept a fishing line attached to it so he could get it back. The sails swelled and the boat started moving.

I grinned. "She looks awesome," I told Kevin.

Suddenly something hit the water with a big

splash. Kevin's boat tipped over on its side. There was another big splash and then another.

"Hey!" I yelped. "What's going on?"

But even as I said it, I knew. Someone was throwing rocks at Kevin's boat!

Chapter 8

I turned around. There, standing right behind me, were Corey Wilson and Ted Stern. "Look at the babies sailing their little boat," Corey sneered.

I felt my face go hot. I knew it probably did look pretty childish: two sixth-graders getting all excited about sailing a toy boat. But Kevin had built the boat himself. It had taken him hours and hours, and he was proud of it.

I clenched my hands into fists. "So?" I said.

"So nothing," Ted chuckled. "You guys are total nerds. And now your stupid boat is getting fire-bombed." He chucked another rock at Kevin's boat. It landed with a crunch against the hull.

"Stop it!" Kevin shouted furiously.

"Oh, wow, we'd better stop. Kevin's upset," Corey said.

"Yeah, he's going to cry 'cause his toy boat got sunk."

Kevin ignored them. He just reeled the sailboat in and scooped it up. The prow was dented, and the white paint on the hull was chipped and scraped.

"I can't you believe you guys are such jerks," I mumbled.

"You want to fight about it?" Corey asked, grinning maliciously.

I gulped. I wanted more than anything to say *yes*. But if I did, Corey Wilson would flatten me. "No, I just want you to go away."

"No problem." Ted grunted. "We don't want to hang around a bunch of dorks with toy sailboats anyway. Do we, Corey?"

"No way." Corey smirked.

The two of them turned and strutted off through the park. Kevin and I stared after them.

"I really hate those guys," I said through clenched teeth. "I wish I could demolish them!"

"Let it go, Matt," Kevin said tiredly. "They're just bullies."

"But you heard all those names they called us— nerds, dorks, babies. I'd like to show them who's a baby." I clenched my fists tighter.

"I'm telling you, Matt, don't get upset about it. They're not worth it."

I stopped and stared at Kevin. "But they wrecked your boat. I can't believe you don't care."

Kevin looked down at his dented boat. "Of course I care," he answered quietly. "I care a lot. I just don't think getting revenge on Corey and Ted would change anything. In their minds we'll always be nerds, and nothing we do will change that."

"A knuckle sandwich might make them think again."

"Look, people always make fun of people who are different," Kevin said simply. "I know they think I'm a total weirdo because I like to make model boats and sail them in this dinky little pond. So what? I don't care what they think."

"Well, *I* do," I said. I remembered the way Ted and Corey had smiled as they tried to wreck Kevin's boat, and I felt myself getting mad all over again.

"I just wish I could get even with them," I muttered. "Just once."

"Yeah, but it wouldn't change anything," Kevin replied. He looked up at the sky. The sun was sinking behind the treetops. "We'd better get going. Remember what your mom said."

"How could I forget," I mumbled gloomily. "'Be home before dark or else!'" I felt as if the whole afternoon had been ruined.

We cut across the park and started down North Adams Street.

Kevin suddenly let out a low whistle. "Hey, look at that."

I turned to follow his gaze. North Adams Street is full of big old mansions. It used to be a really wealthy part of town, but a lot of the rich people who lived there moved out years ago. Some of the houses are pretty shabby now, but the house Kevin was gaping at was the shabbiest by far. It was big and gray with peeling paint and cracked windows. A tall, spiky hedge had grown through the rusting wrought-iron gate that encircled the property. It looked like a haunted house in an old movie.

"It's a big, old house," I said. "So what?"

"Not the house." Kevin pointed. "The sign."

The sign was taped to a dark, dusty window beside the heavy wooden front door. It was hand-lettered, and

I had to squint to read it. When I did, my mouth fell open. "Split-Face Productions!" I exclaimed.

You'd never think of a computer company being in a dusty old house like that—especially not a company that had just made a game as cool as *The Furious Four*. I took a step forward to make sure I wasn't seeing things. I'd imagined that the computer company that had created the coolest new game on the Net would have ultramodern offices. Who would have thought Split-Face Productions would be in a rickety old house?

"Unbelievable," I said. Then I felt a rush of excitement. Meltdown Man had been invented just a few blocks from my house!

"Hey," I said to Kevin excitedly. "Maybe we should ring the doorbell and say hi. Tell whoever is in there that we're big fans of the game."

Kevin hesitated. "I don't know," he mumbled, glancing around nervously. "It's getting kind of dark."

It was, and even I had to admit the house looked pretty creepy in the long twilight shadows. Still, I didn't want to just leave. I put my hand on the gate and started forward. Kevin followed me. I heard a screech and jumped as a scrawny black cat raced across the path in front of me and disappeared into the dark, thorny hedge.

"Matt, come on. Let's not go in there!" Kevin pleaded.

"Why not? What could happen?" I demanded. But I was starting to feel scared, too. It was like the old house was warning me not to come any closer. Then I thought of how impressed Corey and Ted would be if they saw me now. I took another step forward. Beside me, Kevin reached out and grabbed my arm. I looked up and froze.

Two eyes were watching us from one of the upstairs windows. It was too dark to see the face of the person they belonged to, but the eyes gleamed with a red glow in the last rays of sunlight.

They didn't look like a person's eyes. They looked like the eyes of Meltdown Man!

Suddenly a sound came rolling out of the open window. It began as a low growl. Slowly, slowly it grew until we could hear it clearly—horribly evil, mocking laughter.

Chapter 9

I felt paralyzed. I could hear Kevin's footsteps pounding away. I knew I should run, too. Instead, I continued to stare up at the window. Suddenly, the eyes disappeared. There was only a thick, dark curtain flapping lightly against the dusty glass.

I swallowed. Then I turned and dashed after Kevin.

"I told you we shouldn't go in there!" Kevin shouted. He looked pale as he clutched the box containing his model boat tight against his chest. I couldn't believe Kevin was so scared. This kid had watched every monster movie on TV for the last three years without even blinking. At our first Boy Scout camp out, he'd even scared away a bear by banging two empty soda cans together.

"I don't know why you're so upset," I said coolly. "Maybe whoever lives there saw something funny when he looked out the window."

"Split-Face lives there," Kevin said softly.

"He's not Split-Face. That's just the name of his company," I replied. "Anyway, I think I'll go back and say hi. Maybe tomorrow."

"I wouldn't."

"Why not? He invented a cool game, whoever he is. I just want to tell him how much I like it."

Now that I was away from the house, it didn't seem nearly so spooky. In fact, I was sure that if I went back there in bright daylight, it wouldn't scare me at all. I had to meet the guy who'd invented the greatest computer game I'd ever played.

"Well, I won't go with you," Kevin declared.

"I can't believe you're being such a chicken about this," I said impatiently. Then I glanced up at Kevin's face. It wasn't fair to give him a hard time when his new model boat had just been ruined. "Sorry, Kevin. I didn't mean that. I know you're not chicken," I corrected myself quickly. "But I still want to go back."

"What for?" Kevin asked.

"I just want to meet the guy who invented Meltdown Man," I answered as we came up to my house.

But that wasn't the only reason I wanted to go back. I was still thinking about Corey and Ted. I was sure they would both be way too scared to go inside a spooky old house like that. If I went back and actually made it inside, I could prove to those two creeps that I wasn't a nerd.

"Well, see you tomorrow," Kevin said as we stood at the end of the driveway. "Maybe we can walk to school together. Chris and I will pick you up."

"Okay," I agreed.

Kevin started down the sidewalk as if he were in a hurry to get home. I couldn't blame him. It hadn't exactly been the greatest afternoon.

"Hey, Kevin, how about we get together on the Net

after dinner?" I called after him, hoping to cheer him up. "We could play another game of *The Furious Four.*"

Kevin stopped and shook his head. "Nah, I don't think so, Matt. I'll play something else if you want, but I think I'd like to give that game a rest for a while."

"You can be Meltdown Man," I offered.

"No, thanks. I'm just not that into it," he mumbled.

I'm not that into sailing model boats, but I do it because you like to, I thought. I knew I was being kind of a jerk, but I couldn't help feeling mad and resentful. We had found the coolest computer game ever, but Kevin didn't want to play it. What was his problem?

"See you tomorrow," Kevin said quickly.

"Later," I replied, scowling.

I stomped into the house in a bad mood. Luckily, Mom had ordered my favorite dinner—pizza topped with ham and pineapple. I know, I know, it sounds gross, but trust me, it's really delicious. My dad was cracking hysterical jokes as we ate. Even Crystal was being less of a pest than usual. By the time dinner was over, I was feeling a lot better.

"Hey, Mom, is it okay if I go on-line for a while?" I asked.

"Did you do your homework?"

"Yes," I lied. Actually, I didn't have much homework for a change.

"Okay, as long as you wash the dishes first."

"Why do I always have to do the dishes?" I moaned. But it was no big deal. All I had to do was load them in the dishwasher and wash a couple of pans.

Fifteen minutes later I sat down at my computer. I thought about trying to get in touch with Chris. He'd said he might be into a game later. Then I shook my head. I didn't feel up to a big challenge game with Chris over who got to be Meltdown Man from now on—especially since I had won the right to be Meltdown Man already.

On the other hand, that meant I had no friends to play with. Then I smiled. That was the great thing about the Internet. You could make new friends any time. There were probably hundreds of kids like me out there dying to play an awesome new game like *The Furious Four.*

"So long as I get to be Meltdown Man," I murmured to myself. I quickly logged on to the Net and went to *http://www/sfp/furiousfour.* Strange. No one else was playing.

I was totally disappointed. Then I thought, *It's not like I really need anyone else to play against. In fact, it's almost better that there isn't anyone.*

I clicked my mouse though the introduction to the game and then selected Meltdown Man as my character.

Instantly, I *was* Meltdown Man. Pounding on my keyboard, I sent Meltdown zinging across the screen. It felt great to be a superhero. Meltdown leaped around, swerving to avoid the mines, man-eating crocodiles, and fierce baboons that guarded Dirk Zorsan's fortress. I thought of how Corey and Ted would look if I could do all this stuff in real life. They'd be scared out of their minds.

One of the best things about *The Furious Four* was that it hadn't been the same any of the times I'd played it. This time Meltdown accidentally stepped into a hidden pit of vipers. It took every ounce of skill I had to get him out of there alive. He had to use not only his laser vision but a new superpower I discovered—his magic melting touch. The vipers were soon reduced to a pile of ash.

Meltdown climbed out of the pit and strode across the drawbridge to the door of Dirk's fortress. He turned his gaze on the lock. It flamed and melted.

Now I was inside . . .

It was pitch black in there—creepy, crawly pitch black. I was sure Dirk Zorsan was lurking somewhere, just waiting for me.

"Lights out!" I heard Mom shout up the stairs.

"In a minute," I grumbled.

That was when it happened. All of a sudden, I felt two hands around my neck—hands clothed in thick, scaly leather.

I was concentrating so hard that it took me a whole second to realize the hands weren't part of the game. They were real. Two leather hands were around my neck, squeezing and squeezing.

They were Dirk Zorsan's hands!

Chapter 10

I tried to scream, but my voice was gone. "Help," I gasped.

That's when someone started giggling. I knew that giggle. Crystal. I reached up and pulled the leather hands away from my neck and whirled around.

My little sister was standing there, laughing at me. On her hands were a pair of my dad's old leather driving gloves.

"Crystal! What do you think you're doing? You almost strangled me to death!" I exclaimed angrily.

"You mean I almost scared you to death," Crystal replied. "I can't believe you're such a fraidy-cat!"

I could feel my cheeks burning. I guess all little sisters are a pain, but Crystal is the biggest pain in the universe. What made it worse was that she was right. I had been scared out of my mind.

I couldn't believe I had really thought that Crystal was the archvillain Dirk Zorsan. "Get out of my room," I growled.

Crystal snickered. "Make me."

It's like a game with Crystal. She teases me and teases me until I get so mad I explode. Then I get in trouble. Mom and Dad have told me a million times to ignore her, but it never works.

"I said 'Get out,'" I repeated furiously.

Crystal stuck her tongue out at me. "I won't," she said. Then she grinned. "Anyway, you're not supposed to be playing that dumb computer game anymore. Mom said lights out, remember? I'm going to tell."

I turned back to my computer screen and tried to shut out the sound of her voice.

Crystal just started to giggle again. "You should have seen your face, Matt! Your eyes looked like they were going to pop out of your head."

"That's it! You're out of here!" I lunged out of my chair and tore after her.

Crystal raced out of my room and started down the hall. "Mom! Dad! Help!" she squealed. "Matt's chasing me!"

I reached out and grabbed the collar of her nightgown.

"Kids, what's going on up there?" I looked down to see my dad peering up at me over the banister.

"Nothing, Dad." I let Crystal go.

"That's a lie! Matt was about to squeeze me to death!" Crystal shouted.

"Matt!" My mom's head poked up over the banister next to my dad's. "Why can't you be nicer to your little sister? Why are you always trying to hurt Crystal?"

"Hurt Crystal?" I burst out indignantly. "She snuck into my room and practically strangled me. She put on your old gloves, Dad, and pretended to be a monster. I could have had a heart attack!"

Dad glowered up at Crystal. "Is that true?"

"Sort of," Crystal mumbled.

"I see." Mom sighed loudly. "Well, I'm getting pretty tired of you two constantly fighting. When I was a little girl . . ."

Crystal and I exchanged a quick glance. When Mom starts a sentence with the words *When I was a little girl,* it usually means we're in for a big lecture. But tonight Mom just shook her head. "Never mind. I'm too tired to get into this. Crystal, apologize to your brother. Matt, apologize to your sister."

"Sorry," Crystal said so my parents could hear. But then she added under her breath, "Fraidy-cat!"

"I'm sorry, too," I said loudly. "But I'll get you later," I whispered.

Crystal looked scared for a moment. Then she stuck her tongue out at me. "No, you won't—Fraidy-cat!"

"Now, everyone to bed," Dad ordered. "It's getting late."

I padded down the hall to my room. My computer was still on. The screen glowed in the dim light. I sat on my bed. I knew I should turn the machine off and go to sleep. But on the other hand, why not play one more quick game?

I'd be in big trouble if Mom or Dad came down the hall to check on me, but they probably wouldn't. They were both pretty tired. Dad had put on a big sales presentation at work, and Mom had showed three houses. She works as a real estate agent when she's not taking care of us. I was pretty sure all my parents wanted to do was go to bed.

I peered at the computer screen. Meltdown's face peered back at me, underneath the words *Game Over.*

The good side of his face looked like it was smiling. Then his mouth moved. I wasn't sure, but I could swear he was saying, "Come on!"

A chill went up my spine. I was definitely losing it. Video-game characters didn't talk to you. They were just programs, right? But then I looked up and was sure I saw Meltdown wink at me. "Come on!" he repeated.

I got up and moved my chair closer to my desk. The next thing I knew I was bent over my computer, my fingers tapping the keys faster and faster. . . .

Chapter 11

I almost slammed into the solid steel wall. Dirk Zorsan's feet thudded close behind me. Any minute now, I would feel his leather-gloved hands tightening around my throat.

"Meltdown, give up! There is no escape," he hissed.

"Never," I whispered back. I had Zorsan's secret formula in my pocket. With it, I could destroy his evil power forever. But first I had to find a way out of the fortress.

I gazed at the high wall in front of me. It was solid steel, three feet thick, and so high I couldn't even see to the top.

There was no way around it. I was trapped!

Then I felt rage stir inside me. I was a freak. Half my face was hideously scarred, thanks to the man chasing me. Dirk Zorsan had wrecked my life. If I let him, he would wreck the lives of all the people on the planet.

My eyes began to tingle and burn. Once again I turned my gaze to the wall—Meltdown's only possible escape.

The wall began to glow an eerie blue. Then it burst

into flames. As I felt Dirk Zorsan's razored gloves rake across my back, I pushed myself through the ring of fire before me.

I felt myself falling into ice-cold blackness.

"Hey, Matt, get up. Your alarm's been going off for the last fifteen minutes. It's driving me bananas!"

I blinked and saw Crystal standing over me. She was already dressed for school. She even had her heart-shaped backpack over her shoulders.

"Uh, what time is it?"

Crystal smirked at me. "Eight o'clock, you dork. If you don't get up and get dressed in a hurry, you're going to be in big trouble."

"Yeah, well, thanks for the warning."

"No problem, moron." Crystal turned and left the room. I could hear her skipping down the hall.

I groaned loudly. Eight o'clock? How late had I stayed up, anyway? I couldn't remember. But one thing was for sure: I felt like I'd been run over by a ten-ton truck.

I rubbed my eyes and stared at my computer screen. It shone with a cold, eerie glow, despite the warm sunlight streaming through the windows. I fumbled out of bed and yanked the shades down. Normally I like the sun, but that morning it made my head ache.

"Matt, are you dressed yet?" Mom called up the stairs. She sounded majorly annoyed. "Your breakfast is getting cold."

"Coming!" I shouted, making a face. My mom is a big believer in eating a healthy breakfast, and she thinks oatmeal is the healthiest breakfast there is. "Terrific," I muttered aloud. "A delicious bowl of cold oatmeal."

I pulled a clean T-shirt over my head and winced. Strangely, all my muscles ached—as if I'd been running for my life the night before instead of just playing a computer game. I squinted at the screen. I couldn't believe I'd forgotten to turn my computer off the night before. I tried to recall what had happened. But all I could remember was leaning over the keyboard and starting another game of *The Furious Four*.

A shiver crept up my spine. It hadn't felt like a game last night. I felt as if I truly were Meltdown Man. I couldn't remember the game ever stopping.

I screwed up my eyes and pulled the curtains across my shaded window. Not only did my muscles ache, but something strange was happening to my eyes. Whenever the sunlight hit them, they stung badly. *Just like Meltdown Man's eyes must feel ever since he was burned by Dirk Zorsan in that chemical blast,* I thought.

"Matt!" This time it was my dad calling up the stairs.

"I said I'm coming!" I yelled as I tugged my jeans over my legs. Scooping my backpack off the floor, I realized guiltily that I'd been so busy playing *The Furious Four* last night, I hadn't even started my math homework. Oh, well, maybe I could do it before class—if my eyes started to feel better.

I stepped into the hall. Ouch! The bright sunlight streaming through the skylight made me wince.

"Matt, hurry up!" Mom was reaching her boiling point.

I started down the stairs, wondering if I should tell my mom how crummy I was feeling. Maybe I had the flu. Sore limbs and scratchy eyes were definitely symptoms of the flu, weren't they? Or was it just that I'd stayed up too late playing computer games?

That's what Mom would say. If I didn't want a lecture, it was best to say nothing.

"Bye, Matt. See you tonight," Dad called out. I waved as he slipped out the front door. Then I had to stop and rub my eyes again. By now my oatmeal was probably ice cold. Talk about a yucky breakfast!

I continued down the stairs faster. Suddenly I felt something hard and round under my left foot. I slipped and went flying through the air, landing in a crumpled heap in the center of the downstairs foyer.

"Owww!" I moaned, lifting my head. Big mistake! The morning sunlight was streaming through the long, narrow windows on either side of the front door. It burned my eyes like hot coals.

"Argggh!" I moaned louder.

"Matt, are you all right?" Mom called from the kitchen.

"I think so," I murmured weakly. I wiggled my arms and legs to make sure nothing was broken.

Crystal was bending over me. "He said he's okay, Mom," she shouted. "Then stop acting like such a baby," Crystal said to me. "I was scared you were really hurt."

"I almost was!" I retorted. "I was coming down the stairs and I slipped—" I broke off. Out of the corner of my eye, I saw what I'd slipped on. Crystal's doll, Sherri.

It's funny. Crystal likes to think she's so grown-up

for her age. But she loves dolls—especially Sherri. Crystal almost acts like Sherri is a real person. She puts her to bed, carries her around everywhere, and even pretends to feed her.

Pretty childish for a third-grader, right?

Anyway, Sherri was always lying around the house. And this time Crystal had left her in the middle of the stairs.

"I tripped on that dumb doll of yours," I continued furiously. I glared at the doll. Sherri has white-blonde hair and big, staring blue eyes. She looks really stupid, even for a doll. "Please don't leave your mutant baby in the middle of the stairs anymore, okay?"

Crystal's lower lip wobbled. "Sherri is not a mutant baby. Anyway, why don't you just watch where you're going?"

"I was watching!"

"No, you weren't," Crystal countered. "You were thinking about your stupid computer games, as usual."

I sat up. "I was not!"

"Were, too!"

I scowled at my sister. Now that I wasn't facing the sun, my eyes had stopped stinging so much. Crystal picked up Sherri and hugged her tight.

"Poor baby!" she crooned.

Poor baby? What about me? I reached out and grabbed Sherri. "Give me that stupid doll," I growled. "I'll stick her somewhere where she won't ever trip me up again."

"Leave her alone! She's mine!" Crystal squealed. She gave a hard tug on Sherri, sending me stumbling backward. I landed flat on the floor again.

"Yow!" I yelped. I glared up at Crystal and Sherri. The doll stared back at me with her blank blue eyes.

I noticed then that my own eyes were throbbing worse than ever. And I was really mad. "That doll has got to go!" I shouted. Only the voice didn't sound like mine. It was deep and grown-up sounding.

"Matt?" Crystal said, staring at me. But I was looking at Sherri. I remembered the steel wall of Dick Zorsan's fortress—how it had turned blue just before it burst into flames. I smiled, imagining how my sister would look if that happened to her dumb doll. Then I stopped smiling.

"Matt, what is it? Matt?" Then Crystal looked down at Sherri and let out a shriek. "Matt! What have you done to her?"

I couldn't say anything. I was too shocked by what was happening. The doll's face was melting right before my eyes! Where her nose had been, there was only an ugly, charred black hole. I gaped as one of Sherri's blue glass eyes popped out of her head.

"Stop it! Please, Matt, stop it!" Crystal sobbed.

"What's going on here?" I turned to see Mom standing in the kitchen doorway.

"It's Sherri," Crystal wailed. "Matt . . . killed her!" She held up the doll. Sherri looked totally gruesome!

Chapter 12

Mom stared at Sherri in horror. "What happened?" she gasped. She turned on me. "Matt Harper, did you do this to your sister's doll?"

I kept my eyes riveted to the floor so I wouldn't have to look at Sherri's horribly twisted features. "No . . . no, I didn't do anything," I stuttered. That was the truth, wasn't it? I *had* been thinking about Meltdown Man and his laser vision, but there was no way I could have fried Sherri like that just by looking at her. Was there?

I shivered.

"Tell me exactly what happened," I heard Mom say to Crystal. Her voice sounded far away.

"I don't know," Crystal whimpered. "Matt tripped over Sherri, and we got in a fight. And then when I looked at her, she was—" She broke off and burst into loud, ragged sobs.

Mom put her arms around Crystal. Then she eyed me over my sister's head. "Matt, are you positive you had nothing to do with this? Because if this is supposed to be some kind of joke, it isn't funny."

I gulped. "Mom, it definitely isn't a joke," I whispered. I still didn't dare to look up.

Mom considered Sherri's distorted face. "Then I don't understand," she murmured. "How could a doll just melt?" She hugged Crystal tighter.

At that moment, I heard the doorbell ringing. It was Kevin and Chris. I'd totally forgotten we'd agreed to walk to school together that morning.

Mom sighed. "It looks like your friends are here, Matt," she said grimly. "And you haven't even had breakfast." She glanced at the door. "I guess you'd better get going. But before you do, don't you think you should tell me about this?"

Crystal lifted her tear-stained face. "Yeah, Matt," she said accusingly. "Tell us how you killed Sherri."

My heart started beating faster. "I . . ." My voice dried up in my throat. What could I say? *Mom, Crystal, I didn't mean to do it, but maybe I melted Sherri's face by staring at it?*

"I swear I don't know how it happened," I said aloud.

Mom sighed again. "Okay, but your father and I will want to talk to you about this some more tonight. And Matt—take some of your allergy medicine. Your eyes look terrible!"

I nodded. Then I turned and ran upstairs to the bathroom. All the way up the stairs, I could hear Crystal's sobs. It made me feel horribly guilty, but I couldn't understand why.

I wasn't responsible for what happened to Sherri, I kept telling myself. *Nobody could destroy a doll just by staring at it.* Then I caught my breath. Nobody but Meltdown Man.

I thought of that pale kid I'd met in the hallway.

Stop playing before it's too late, he'd said. I'd thought he was just jealous because he wanted to be Meltdown Man. But maybe I was wrong. Maybe he was trying to warn me.

But warn me about what?

A terrifying thought came creeping into my mind. What if what happened to Sherri was only the beginning? What if, somehow, something had happened to me, and now I had Meltdown Man's super powers?

But that was impossible!

With shaking fingers, I grabbed the bottle of allergy medicine off the bathroom shelf. Suddenly I caught sight of myself in the oval mirror above the sink and let out a strangled cry. My eyes were bright red. Just like Meltdown Man's!

There was no way I could go to school looking like that. I blundered out into the hall, desperately wondering what to do. A pair of Dad's old sunglasses were lying on the hall table. I picked them up and shoved them on. Kids might laugh at me, but at least now no one would see my blood-red eyes.

Then I noticed that my eyes had stopped stinging and burning. They felt much better with the sunglasses on.

I bolted down the stairs. Kevin and Chris were waiting for me by the front door.

"Hey, check out the shades," Kevin exclaimed.

"What's with the new look, Matt?" Chris asked.

"It's nothing," I muttered. "Come on. Let's go."

"Bye, Matt," Mom said softly behind me. Crystal sniffed loudly.

"Bye, Mom. Bye, Crystal. See you this afternoon," I replied quickly. I tried to make my voice sound normal, but it didn't. It sounded high and squeaky and scared.

Mom gave me a concerned look. "We'll talk more after school," she said.

"Yeah, sure."

I practically ran out the front door. Chris and Kevin had to sprint to catch up with me.

"Hey, what's your hurry?" Kevin said. "We're not late."

"Yeah, but I need to get to school early this morning," I lied. "I have something to take care of—an overdue book at the library."

"Oh," Kevin said.

Then I noticed Chris was staring at me. "Hey, Matt, those shades are really something," he declared. Before I could take a step back, he reached out and yanked them off my face.

Ouch! The morning sunlight felt like fire against my eyeballs. "Hey, give me back my glasses!" I yelped.

But now Kevin was staring at me, too. "Matt, what's wrong with your eyes? They're so red!"

"It's nothing," I mumbled. "Just allergies."

Kevin nodded. He knew I had bad allergies. "What a bummer," he commented. "The pollen must be extra bad this year."

"It is," I told him. Chris was dangling my sunglasses over my head. He had a mischievous grin on his face. "Come on, Chris," I pleaded. "Give me back my shades, please?"

But he only held them higher. "What'll you give me for them?" he teased.

"Come on, Chris," Kevin protested. "Can't you see he's got allergies?"

"Allergies, huh?" Chris's grin widened. "Are you sure it's allergies, Matt? Or have you been spending too much time in front of your computer? You know what, Matt? With those red eyes, you look just like Meltdown Man!"

"Chris, cut it out!" I was suddenly scared and mad, too. Why was Chris torturing me like this? Had he guessed what was happening to me? "Just give me back my shades. Now!"

My voice must have sounded really sharp because Kevin's eyes widened. "I think you'd better give Matt his glasses, Chris," he said firmly.

Chris stopped grinning. "Okay, okay, I was just trying to have a little fun," he grumbled.

I snatched the glasses out of his hand and pulled them over my burning eyes. Instant relief.

"Your eyes do look like Meltdown Man's, though," Chris added half under his breath. "I've never seen eyes that red."

"I told you, I have really bad allergies." I faked a sneeze and a sniffle.

"Or else you're turning into Meltdown Man," Chris joked again.

My heart sank. *Chris just isn't going to leave it alone,* I thought hopelessly. What was his problem, anyway? Why did he always have to give me a hard time? If it weren't for Kevin, I would never have been Chris's friend.

I glared at Chris angrily from behind my shades. Then a wave of terror passed over me. If it really was me who melted Crystal's doll, I probably could melt down anything—*even a person!* In the game, whenever Meltdown Man got mad, he got dangerous.

Could that be true for me as well?

I put my backpack over my shoulders and started walking fast. "Come on," I said. "I told you guys I have to get to school early."

Kevin and Chris exchanged a glance. Then they followed me down the sidewalk. It was a warm, sunny morning, but I felt chilled all over. It was all I could do to keep my teeth from chattering. I kept thinking of the strange kid I'd met in the hallway. *Stop while there's still time,* he'd told me. But I hadn't listened. I remembered how, the last time I saw him, he'd just shaken his head at me sadly. *Too late,* he'd mouthed. And then I remembered that he was always wearing sunglasses.

One thing was certain—I had to find that kid in a hurry. Maybe he could help me figure out what was going on.

Chapter 13

"This is a difficult problem, Matt," said the principal's secretary, Mrs. Willis. "You say you don't know his name? Or what class he's in?"

"Uh, no," I faltered. "But I'm pretty sure he's in sixth grade, like me."

I was in the school office. I'd left Kevin and Chris the minute we walked through the front gate. I'd told them I had to get to the library right away. Instead, I went to see Mrs. Willis. I was trying to track down that kid who'd warned me against playing *The Furious Four*.

I had told Mrs. Willis that the kid, whoever he was, had accidentally taken my math notebook at lunch the day before. "I have to find him as soon as I can, because we have math class second period," I explained desperately.

Mrs. Willis nodded. "Of course, Matt, I understand." She peered at me across her desk and frowned. "Are you sure you want to keep those sunglasses on inside?" she asked kindly. "It must be kind of hard to see."

"Yeah, but . . . I have to keep them on," I stammered nervously. "My eyes are bugging me. Allergies."

"You should get some eyedrops."

"I know, but I didn't have time. They came on all of a sudden while I was walking to school this morning."

"Oh, dear," Mrs. Willis said. She wrinkled up her forehead. "Well, I don't quite know how to find this boy for you, Matt. Thin, pale, brown hair. I'm afraid that describes a lot of students at our school."

Suddenly she smiled. "Wait! I know. Why don't you see if you can track him down in last year's yearbook?" She took a yearbook down from the bookshelf behind her. "If he's a sixth-grader like you, he would have been a fifth-grader last year."

"Great idea!" I almost grabbed the yearbook out of her hand and started flipping through it. Then I saw him. It was definitely him. Only he looked heavier, healthier, in the picture than he had in real life. "Scott Grady," I read aloud. "That's him."

"Scott Grady?" Mrs. Willis's round pink face turned white as a piece of chalk. "But, Matt, that's impossible! Scott Grady transferred out of here last year. He went to Tolland—you know, across town. And then . . ." She bit her lip.

"Then what?" I blurted. I felt a cold finger of fear stab into me.

"He disappeared," Mrs. Willis replied weakly. "Don't you know, Matt? He's the boy that's missing. It's in all the papers. Scott Grady left school one afternoon but never arrived home. Everyone in town has been searching for him. They haven't found him, though," Mrs. Willis finished sadly.

"He disappeared?" I stammered.

So that was why the kid had looked so familiar

when I first saw him in the school hallway! I remembered where I'd seen his face now. I couldn't understand why I hadn't made the connection before. I'd seen the posters about Scott Grady everywhere. And Mom mentioned his disappearance practically every time Crystal or I left the house.

The blood drained from my face. "That's awful," I whispered.

That was a major understatement. If Scott Grady had disappeared off the face of the earth, what was he doing in my school talking to me? And why was I the only person who had seen him?

I looked up to see Mrs. Willis eyeing me. "Matt, are you certain you saw Scott Grady?" she asked anxiously. "Where did you see him exactly?"

"I—it couldn't have been him. I guess I must have made a mistake."

Mrs. Willis frowned. "But you picked out his picture. You said that he was the boy who took your notebook. Listen, Matt, if you really saw Scott Grady, I think we ought to get in touch with the police at once!"

"No!" I almost shouted. "It was a mistake. I made a mistake—that's all!"

Just then the bell rang. I'd never been so relieved to hear the bell in my life. "Thanks for your help," I said quickly. "But I'm sure it wasn't him who took my notebook. It must have been someone else. I just got confused when I saw his picture—that's all."

I turned and ran out of the office. I could feel Mrs. Willis staring after me, but I didn't look back.

How could I tell her—or anyone—what was going on?

Scott Grady had disappeared a few days ago. Where had he gone? Had he run away because the same thing that was happening to me had happened to him? His disappearance had to have something to do with *The Furious Four.* Otherwise, why would he come to me, why would he tell me to stop playing before it was too late?

I thought of how weird and pale Scott Grady had looked—almost transparent. Then an even more horrible thought occurred to me. What if Scott Grady was really gone? Like dead? What if the Scott Grady I'd met was a ghost?

Chapter 14

I slunk into homeroom just as the late bell rang. Mrs. Feldman was telling everyone about how great the upcoming Harvest Fair was going to be. There was going to be a hayride, a tunnel of mirrors, and a ton of booths with food and crafts. "And for all you monster fans out there," Mrs. Feldman finished, "we're going to have a really spooky haunted house with some of the most gruesome monsters you've ever seen."

"Great!" everyone said.

Yeah, great, I thought. It did sound great. At least, normally I would have thought it did. But I was too wrapped up in my own problems. My eyes were still stinging. I still didn't feel right.

And now I had Scott Grady to worry about.

"Life couldn't possibly get any worse," I said under my breath. Boy, was I ever wrong.

As soon as Mrs. Feldman finished talking, everyone stood up and started shuffling out of the classroom. "Hey, where's everyone going?" I blurted out. Then I remembered. Today we had gym first period. I had to face Mr. Allen wearing sunglasses. This was going to be very bad.

I wondered desperately if I could go to the school nurse and tell her I wasn't feeling well. But then I'd have to take off my glasses, and she'd see my eyes. Mrs. Jakeway was a great nurse. I knew she'd figure out that more than just plain old allergies were bothering me. This plan would never work.

"Hey, Matt, hurry up!" Kevin said, clapping me on the back. "We don't want Mr. Allen to get on our case!"

I looked up at him. Kevin was smiling. I couldn't believe how normal he was acting. It was amazing. He didn't seem to have any idea that I wasn't my usual old self.

Matt "Fumble-Fingers" Harper.

"You mean, you don't want him to get on our case any more than usual," I corrected him, forcing myself to sound as normal as he did. "When has Mr. Allen ever *not* gotten on our case?"

Kevin chuckled. "That's the truth—especially my case. He thinks it's unnatural that someone as tall as me doesn't want to play basketball."

"At least he thinks you have potential," I said. "I'm just a hopeless shrimp as far as Mr. Allen is concerned."

We walked down to the gym locker room. Chris was there waiting for us. He was already changed and ready to go. I pulled on my sweatpants and sweatshirt as fast as I could.

"Hey, Matt, you're not going to wear your shades out there, are you?" Chris demanded.

"Yeah." Kevin frowned. "I don't think Mr. Allen is going to go for you wearing sunglasses."

"I don't have a choice," I replied in a low voice. "These allergies are killing me."

Chris and Kevin exchanged a look. Then they both shrugged, and we filed out into the gym.

Mr. Allen always makes us line up in order of height. I hate that, because Kevin and I are always on opposite ends of the line.

I took my place. My heart was pounding faster and faster. To calm myself down, I stared at my feet.

I knew what was coming. I was hoping Mr. Allen wouldn't say anything about my glasses, but I was ninety-nine percent sure that he would. I waited for the disaster to happen.

It didn't take long.

"Harper, what's with the movie-star shades?" Mr. Allen boomed.

I kept my head down.

"Harper, take 'em off—now!"

I lifted my head.

"I can't, Mr. Allen. I have these bad allergies, see, and my eyes are stinging, and—"

"Look, Fumble-Fingers, I'm not asking you to take those ridiculous sunglasses off. I'm ordering you to take them off. So take them off. Got it?"

I didn't move. I could hear Mr. Allen's footsteps coming closer and closer—just like Dirk Zorsan chasing Meltdown Man. Then I saw my gym teacher's big hand reach toward my face. I don't think I'd ever hated him as much as I did at that moment.

His hand grasped the sunglasses and tore them off. "Harper," Mr. Allen growled. "I ought to send you to the principal for this."

I staggered backward as the bright sunlight cut through my eyes like sharp knives. "Sir, my sunglasses! I need my sunglasses!"

"Mr. Harper, your sunglasses have just been confiscated." Mr. Allen stuck them in his shirt pocket. That's when it happened. My hand reached out, and before I could stop myself, I grabbed the sunglasses out of his pocket.

Mr. Allen looked totally shocked for a moment. Then he started shouting. He told me to take myself to the principal's office immediately. He said he was going to make sure I was suspended. He also said I could forget about passing gym. "In fact, Harper, you'll be lucky if you ever make it out of sixth grade!" he stormed.

I could hear every word Mr. Allen said, but it all sounded like it was coming from far away. At least I had my shades back. I needed them, too. My eyes were burning more than ever. I started to put the glasses on.

"Harper, stop right there!" Mr. Allen bellowed. He reached out for my glasses again. I took a step back.

"I want those glasses now!" he shouted.

I looked up at my gym teacher. His face was beet red. He looked like he was about to explode—like I'd committed the crime of the century or something. I felt myself getting mad. Very mad.

It's not fair, I thought. *He's just a big bully.*

Then my eyes started to tingle. I knew what was coming, but I didn't know how to stop it.

I stared at Mr. Allen with my blazing red eyes.

A puff of smoke began to rise around his feet. Mr.

Allen began to fade, to melt like a giant plastic doll. Suddenly there was a little burst of blue flame. And then it was over.

Mr. Allen was gone.

My gym teacher had disappeared.

He had suffered a total meltdown!

Chapter 15

It was the most terrible moment of my life. I'd made my gym teacher melt, vanish—maybe even killed him.

I stared in dismay at the space where Mr. Allen had been. I wished I could disappear, too. The other kids were looking around, confused expressions on their faces.

"Hey, where did Mr. Allen go?" Corey Wilson exclaimed. "Fumble-Fingers, did you see where he went?"

"Uh, no!" I could barely speak. I put my sunglasses on to ease the painful burning feeling in my eyes.

I expected Corey or one of the others to say something. *What are you talking about, Harper? He was talking to you, and then all of a sudden he melted!* But they didn't. They all just started calling, "Hey, Mr. Allen? Where are you? Mr. Allen!"

None of them even looked in my direction. I suddenly realized that they didn't think I had anything to do with our gym teacher's disappearance. Even though they'd seen Mr. Allen melt right in front of their eyes, they didn't believe it had happened.

Or maybe they hadn't seen him melt. Maybe I was the only one who knew.

"Hey, Mr. Allen, where are you?" they all shouted.

There was no answer.

"This is weird," Chris said.

"Nah," chimed in Ted Stern. "He probably went to his office to cool down."

"Yeah," agreed several of the others.

Corey looked right at me. "Allen's really mad. You're in big trouble now, Fumble-Fingers," he said with a grin.

"No kidding," I mumbled. I still could hardly believe that none of them knew what I had done, even though they'd seen it with their very own eyes. "I guess I'll go to the principal's office."

Kevin's eyes met mine. "You'd better go right now, Matt. You don't want to get in any more trouble with Mr. Allen."

"But where is Mr. Allen?" Ted demanded.

"He must be around here somewhere," Corey said. "I mean, like, the dude can't just have disappeared." Corey sounded scared, which would normally have made me very happy. But not now—not when I knew what I'd done.

"You'd better get going, Matt," Kevin repeated.

I took a deep breath and started toward the gym door. As I slipped into the hall, I could hear the guys behind me still calling out Mr. Allen's name.

I sprinted down the hall, but I didn't go to the principal's office. I headed for the school exit.

Normally I'm the last person on the planet who would ever skip out of school in the middle of the morning. But that was just what I was about to do. The way I saw it, I had no choice. I had to find out what was happening—fast!

I had to know if I was going crazy or if I was really turning into Meltdown Man. Mostly, I had to find out if it was really too late to save Mr. Allen—and myself.

I winced as I jogged across the school parking lot. My gym teacher had always been mean to me and my friends. But I hadn't meant to make him disappear like that. Even thinking about it made me feel sick. It was the worst thing I'd ever seen, the worst thing I'd ever done. It was a million times worse than the time I whacked a baseball right into our next-door neighbor's big picture window and it shattered into a zillion pieces. Worse than the time I accidentally blew up my dad's power drill trying to drill holes in the concrete patio in the backyard.

This time I was in more trouble than I'd ever imagined. I'd melted my gym teacher. And there was no one I could turn to for answers except Scott Grady. But he had disappeared. No one knew where he was or what had happened to him. For all I knew, he might even be a ghost.

My heart hammering, I crept down the street. I didn't even know where I was going. And I was terrified that at any moment someone would spot me. In our town, people are pretty nosy. If anyone I knew saw me, they would definitely want to know why I wasn't in school in the middle of the morning.

I let out a long sigh as I tried to sort through the mess I was in. From what I could tell, I'd turned into Meltdown Man. Crystal's doll was history. And I might have killed Mr. Allen. The only person who could help me had disappeared. There was no one else.

Or was there?

In a flash the answer came to me. There was only one place I could go to find out what was happening to me: the creepy gray house on North Adams. I had to go to Split-Face Productions.

I started to tremble. Now that Kevin wasn't around to impress, there was no way I wanted to go back there alone. It was the scariest-looking house I'd ever seen. But I didn't have a choice.

Just then I heard sirens wailing in the distance. They came closer and closer, then stopped abruptly. I slowly turned my head. Two police cars had pulled up in front of my school.

I didn't need to ask anyone why the police were there. I knew. They had come to find out what had happened to Mr. Allen. And who would be the logical person to question first? The kid who'd been seen arguing with him just moments before he disappeared. Me: Matt Harper!

My heart leaped into my mouth. Suddenly I heard a noise behind me—leaves crunching under someone's foot. I whirled around in a panic, but there was no one there. Still, I couldn't shake the feeling that someone was following me.

I turned back around and streaked down the street as fast as I could.

Chapter 16

I blinked my eyes behind my dark glasses.

I hoped it was just because I was wearing shades, but the gray house looked even scarier in the morning sun than it had the night before. The peeling paint looked like old blisters. The dark, thorny hedges on either side of the walkway looked sharp and menacing—like the spear points that topped the high steel fence around Dirk Zorsan's secret fortress.

The windows of the house were cracked and dirty. Each one was shielded by thick, dark curtains. The front door was painted black. The place reminded me of a tomb.

I peered up at the sign in the window. The words *Split-Face Productions* were printed in dark red ink. When Kevin and I were here yesterday, I hadn't noticed that it looked like dried blood.

I nervously pushed on the rusty iron gate. It swung open with a high-pitched screech. I started slowly up the walk. Dust and old leaves whirled around my feet.

My nose started to itch. *"Kerchoo!"* My sneeze sounded as loud as a firecracker. I heard something stir behind me. It sounded like someone slipping through the gate and slinking up the crooked path after me. I looked over my shoulder.

There was no one there.

I turned to the house again. It looked like an angry face sneering down at me. My teeth started to chatter. I wished I could just run away and never come back. But then I thought about Mr. Allen.

Mr. Allen and Scott Grady.

Whatever happened, I had to keep going. Or else they might never be found.

Slowly I climbed the creaky wooden steps that led up to the black-painted door. I rang the bell. There was no answer.

"Anyone home?" I called. My voice echoed strangely off the warped glass windows. It sounded high and desperate—like the voice of a ghost. I swallowed and waited for a reply.

Still no answer.

"Anyone home?"

All of a sudden, the door burst open. "I've been waiting for you!" growled a raspy voice.

I looked up. Then I started to shake.

In the light of the sun, I could see a man's face peering out at me from the pitch darkness inside the house. Half of it looked normal, but the other half was crisscrossed with angry red and purple scars. Burn marks. It didn't even look like a man's face. It looked like the face of a monster!

Like the face of Meltdown Man.

I gasped and stepped backward. I had to get out of there—fast.

"Never mind," I babbled. "I'll come by some other time."

The mouth on the scarred side of the man's face curled up in a gruesome smile. "Too late!" he whispered. His long arm came swooping out of the doorway. A gigantic hand grabbed me by the shoulder.

"Let me go!" I begged. "Please, let me go!"

But the man with the monster face had pulled me inside the house. In the darkness, the only sound I heard was the door clicking shut behind me.

Chapter 17

"Let go of me!" I shrieked. "Let me go!"

The man didn't say anything.

"Please, you've got to let me go!" I cried.

"But you just got here," he said in a low, menacing voice. "What can I do for you?" His smile was grotesque.

"It's about the game," I croaked. "*The Furious Four.*"

I could see the man's eyes shining in the darkness. The eye on the burned side of his face gleamed brighter. "You liked my game?"

I turned away. This guy's face was beginning to gross me out.

"Yeah. Lots. It's a great game," I squeaked. "There's only one problem. I think . . . I think I'm turning into Meltdown Man. You've got to help me!"

The man began to laugh—a soft, gurgling sound that rose up in his throat. "Why do you need help?" he asked. "I thought you said you liked my game. If you like my game, why don't you want to stay part of it forever?" The way he said *forever* made the hair on the back of my neck rise.

"It's gotten out of control," I explained miserably.

"You don't understand. I made my gym teacher disappear!"

The man leaned closer. His terrible eyes bored deep into mine. "But you wanted him to leave you alone," he said. "Didn't you?"

I opened my mouth, but no sound came out. I stared up at the man with the burned face. Split-Face. That's what Kevin had called him, and he'd been right. Now I knew for sure that this was the guy who'd invented the game.

"Sometimes I did," I replied wretchedly.

Split-Face smiled triumphantly. "Of course you did," he hissed. "You hated the way he picked on you. You wanted revenge, just like me. That's why you played the game."

"Revenge," I repeated with a shudder. *Is that true?* I wondered.

"I don't know," I said aloud. "Maybe. I don't like Mr. Allen. He wasn't—he isn't very nice to me or my friends. But I didn't mean to make him disappear! I never imagined for a second I could make something like that happen."

"But you did!" Split-Face exclaimed. A breeze stirred the black curtains that hung over the windows. A ray of sunlight lit up his hideously scarred face.

"If you want to be a superhero, you have to pay the price," Split-Face went on in a faraway-sounding voice. "Anyway, it's too late to change the past. Nothing can bring him back. Nothing can stop the game. Not even me."

Split-Face pointed at his deformed face. "Just as I can't change back to what I used to be," he added in a raspy whisper. "I am what I am forever!"

It was like he wasn't even talking to me anymore—like he'd forgotten I was there. Yet in some strange way, I understood what he was saying.

His face made him different. Hideous. Scary. There was nothing he could do about that. I almost felt sorry for him for a moment. He must have been in a bad accident for his face to look like that.

But then I remembered what had happened to Mr. Allen and Scott Grady and how Crystal had cried when Sherri melted.

All of those people had been hurt because of the game Split-Face had created. And they hadn't done anything to him.

"But what happened to you has nothing to do with me!" I cried desperately.

Split-Face sneered at me. "Doesn't it?" he said. "Then tell me, why did you like playing the game so much?"

"I don't know. It made me feel . . ." My voice trailed off. "Cooler. Better." I took a deep breath. "When I played your game, it was like I could do things no other kid could do."

Split-Face began to chuckle. "Yes, Matt. And don't you like being better than the other kids?"

A chill went down my spine. How did he know my name?

"You have to stay in the game now, Matt."

I remembered Scott Grady. *Too late,* he'd said. I glanced around the dark house frantically.

"What about Scott Grady?" I asked desperately. "He tried to warn me, but I didn't listen. Then I heard he'd disappeared. Where is he? Is he here? Are you keeping him prisoner here?"

Split-Face chuckled again. "He wanted my help, too. But he's not here now," he murmured. "He's in the game." Another ray of sun from the window lit up his face. He looked like a monster out of my worst nightmares. I cried out in terror and turned to run for the door.

"I'm getting out of here," I shouted. "You're crazy. I'm going to go tell the police."

Split-Face reached out and seized me by the arm. I fought as hard as I could. But he was incredibly strong. "Let me go," I pleaded, my heart pounding faster and faster.

"You can't tell anyone," Split-Face replied flatly. "It will destroy the game. And nothing can destroy the game." Then he dragged me across the room, farther and farther into the darkness.

I thought I was going to faint. Then I saw something glowing in the corner. It was a computer monitor.

I stared at it in wonder.

On the screen were the opening graphics for *The Furious Four*.

Meltdown Man's face peered out at me. His face was a twin of the face beside me. I gazed in horror. I couldn't believe I had ever thought Meltdown Man was a friend, a partner. He was the most hideous creature I'd ever seen.

"See, Matt," Split-Face said gleefully, "thanks to this game, you have become just like me. You and Scott Grady. Soon others will, too."

"What others?" I asked, although I didn't really want to know the answer.

"The others who will play my game. Meltdown Man will live forever!"

Split-Face pushed me down into a chair in front of the screen. "Now, let's play," he said happily.

I stared at him in horror. "No way."

Split-Face frowned. "Play!" he repeated. It was an order. I reached my trembling fingers out toward the keyboard. But before I could hit the keys, I heard something—it sounded like a door opening.

Then a familiar voice shouted, "Matt! Matt, where are you?"

Chapter 18

I whirled around. A dark figure blundered into the room. It was Kevin.

I'd never been so happy to see him. In a flash I realized that Kevin must have followed me from school. Had he guessed what was going on? Or was he just worried because I was acting so strangely?

I almost didn't care. I was just happy to see him—and happy that I wasn't all alone with Split-Face.

Kevin spotted me sitting by the computer. "Come on, Matt, let's get out of here!" he shouted. But he didn't see what I saw. Split-Face was coming up behind him.

"Kevin, watch out!" I yelled. There was no time for him to move. In less than a second, Split-Face had his hands around my best friend's neck.

"Stop! Don't hurt him," I pleaded.

Split-Face let go of Kevin's neck, but he kept a tight grip on my friend's shoulder. "Who is he?" he demanded angrily.

I swallowed. "He's my best friend, Kevin."

Split-Face's eyes flashed at me across the room. "Is he a player of the game?" he asked eagerly.

I hesitated. "He's played the game," I answered. I glanced at Kevin's pale, terrified face. Suddenly I felt horribly guilty. Kevin *had* played *The Furious Four.* But he'd never liked it—not the way I did. And if what Split-Face had said was true, it was because I'd liked the game so much that we were in so much trouble.

Me and Kevin and Scott Grady, wherever he was.

"You've got to let him go," I said, my voice rising. "He's not like me. He played the game, but he didn't care about it. He never wanted to be part of it. Please, just let him go. He won't tell anyone."

Split-Face hesitated. Then his mouth curled up into a sneer. "I can't let him go," he replied in a toneless voice. "If he doesn't like the game, he shouldn't have come here. I don't want to keep him prisoner. But what else can I do? If I let him go, he'll destroy the game. And nothing can destroy the game."

"If you don't let him go, I won't play," I blurted desperately.

Split-Face's eyes narrowed. "But you have to play," he said solemnly. "The game needs you."

"I said I won't, and I won't—unless you let him go!"

Split-Face only tightened his grip on Kevin. "I can't," he snarled. He started walking toward me, dragging Kevin along beside him. "If I let him go, he'll tell someone," he ranted. "He'll destroy the game. And I will never let that happen."

Split-Face's enormous hand closed over my arm. The next thing I knew, he was dragging Kevin and me across the vast, dark room. I knew I should fight, but I also knew it would do no good.

Split-Face was so strong, so terribly strong.

He shoved Kevin and then me through a small doorway. I felt myself falling forward. It felt like I was going to keep falling forever. And above me, I could hear a ghastly sound.

It was the sound of Split-Face's wild laughter.

Chapter 19

I landed with a thud on a hard floor. Groaning, I sat up and gazed into the darkness. Kevin was breathing hard beside me.

"Are you okay?" I whispered.

"I think so," he replied. "Where are we?"

I pulled off my sunglasses. It was amazing that they hadn't broken in the fall. I could now see that we were in a small room with stone walls. The only light came from a tiny chink high in one of the walls.

"I don't know," I answered. "It looks like some kind of dungeon." I peered at the slick stones and shuddered. The place was exactly like one of the underground prison cells in Dirk Zorsan's steel fortress.

Kevin shook his head. "It's not a dungeon," he said. "I think it's a wine cellar. A lot of these old houses had them. That wooden thing over there is a wine rack."

I sighed hopelessly. "Well, it may as well be a dungeon. Because there's no way out of here."

Now that my eyes had adjusted to the light, I could see that the cellar—or whatever it was—was only three or four steps below the first floor. But the only way out was blocked by a thick wooden door.

I crept forward and tested it. It was locked, and it was so thick that there was no way Kevin and I could break through it.

"He can't just leave us here," Kevin said. A note of fear had crept into his voice.

"Yes, he can. He's insane!"

Kevin's eyes went wide. "So we're trapped?"

My mouth felt dry. "Yes," I croaked.

Kevin looked at me. "Why did you come here?" he asked sadly. "What's happening to you, Matt?" He lowered his voice. "I saw what you did to Mr. Allen. I saw how he melted when you stared at him. I didn't want to believe my eyes, but . . ."

Kevin cleared his throat. "It's got something to do with the game, doesn't it?" he asked in a wavering voice. "When I saw you wearing those shades this morning, I knew something weird was going on. And I had this wild idea that somehow you were turning into Meltdown Man. I told myself I was going crazy, but then in gym class, when Mr. Allen . . . disappeared, I knew I was right.

"That's why I followed you," he finished unhappily. "Because I knew you were in big trouble and I wanted to help. But I still don't understand how all of this happened."

"I don't understand myself," I replied in a strangled voice. "I just know Split-Face is behind it. He programmed some kind of weird spell or something into the game. If you play it and you like it . . ." I swallowed. I couldn't bring myself to explain to Kevin *why* I had liked the game so much. "I mean, if you like Meltdown Man, you get sucked into the game somehow. And then you become Meltdown Man for real.

"What I'm trying to say is that you did see what you think you saw. I melted Mr. Allen. I didn't mean to, but"—my voice cracked—"when I get really mad, I can look at something and just melt it. This morning I melted Crystal's doll."

Kevin stared at me. "You're kidding."

"No. I tripped over it on the stairs. Then I got really mad, and, before I knew it, the doll's face was gone."

Suddenly Kevin cracked up. So did I. It might sound nuts to start laughing at a time like that, but there was nothing else we could do. "You melted that stupid doll?" Kevin sputtered.

"Yeah. Her eyes popped out of her head and everything!"

I abruptly stopped laughing. "But you know, it didn't feel good. It's the kind of thing I always wanted to do—really get even with Crystal. But when I melted Sherri, Crystal just cried and cried. And it made me feel awful."

Kevin stopped smiling. "I bet."

"The whole thing is just incredibly creepy," I said.

"Yeah," Kevin agreed solemnly. "I still can't believe you can really melt stuff, Matt. I can't believe you could just look at that door"—he gestured at the heavy door at the top of the steps—"and melt it!"

I lifted my head. Why hadn't I thought of that before?

"Kevin, you're a genius!" I said excitedly. "I *can* just look at that door and melt it! Watch this."

I lifted my head higher and focused on the thick wooden door that held us prisoner.

Chapter 20

I stared at the door as hard as I could. My eyes started to throb. A dazzling ray of light flashed across the room.

Meltdown Man's laser vision.

A blue glow surrounded the door. I concentrated harder. Any minute now, the door was going to burst into flames. Any minute now, Kevin and I were going to be free.

"Amazing!" Kevin breathed.

The blue glow grew brighter and brighter. Then it faded.

"Hey, what happened?" Kevin cried.

I blinked. The door was still there. There was no smoke. There were no flames. The door looked as solid as ever.

"I don't know!" I whispered. "I tried as hard as I could, but it didn't work. Maybe I just need to get madder. It only worked before when I was really mad."

I tried to make myself mad. I thought about what Split-Face had done to Scott Grady. I thought about Mr. Allen and what I'd done to him. Then I thought about Split-Face and how he'd taken us prisoner. There was a chance Split-Face would never let Kevin and me out of there alive.

A white-hot rage passed through me. I fixed my eyes on the door. It began to glow again, but the glow was even weaker than before. It faded quickly.

"I don't understand," I said. "It's not working!"

Dark as it was in the room, my eyes still burned. I picked my sunglasses up off the floor and put them on. I could hardly see, but at least my eyes had stopped stinging.

Kevin didn't say anything, but I knew what he was thinking. If I couldn't melt the door, we were never going to get out of there. We were going to be Split-Face's prisoners forever. Just like Scott Grady.

"Maybe your powers don't work anymore," Kevin said bitterly. "Maybe Split-Face took them away."

"Or maybe I need to play the game again," I said dully. "Maybe the power will get stronger after I play the game."

Then the glimmer of an idea slipped into my head. Maybe the only way to get Kevin and me out of this mess was to agree to play the game. Somehow, I had to get Split-Face to let me play.

I stood up and ran to the top of the short staircase in the corner. Then I banged on the door with my fists as hard as I could.

"Hey, I have to talk to you!" I yelled.

There was a moment of silence. And then I heard a key turning in the lock. The door creaked open.

Split-Face loomed over me, his eyes burning like flames in his scarred face. "What do you want?" he growled viciously.

I opened my mouth. Everything depended on what I said now.

"I—I want to make a deal with you," I stammered.

His eyes narrowed suspiciously. "What kind of deal?"

"You want me to play the game, right?" I whispered.

Split-Face's eyes lit up. Then very slowly he nodded his head. "Yes," he said in a singsong voice. "You should play the game. The game needs you. Meltdown Man needs your anger!"

"Fine," I said quickly. "I'll play. But on one condition. If I win—if Meltdown Man steals Dirk Zorsan's secret formula—you have to let my friend go."

A look of terrible excitement came into Split-Face's eyes. "Meltdown Man has never managed to steal the secret formula," he rasped. "Dirk Zorsan always wins." Then his mouth curved up into a sinister smile. "But Meltdown Man must win in the end," he breathed.

Split-Face thought for a moment. Then he turned his scarred face to me. "If you play the game and steal the secret formula and destroy Dirk Zorsan forever, I will let your friend go."

He stepped back from the door and motioned me forward. I stepped up into the room. My legs felt like wet noodles, but I forced myself to keep walking. After a moment, Kevin followed me.

Like a moth drawn to a flame, I walked toward the glowing computer screen in the corner of the vast, dark room. Meltdown Man's face smiled at me from the screen. I shivered. He was a twin of Split-Face— only bigger and stronger. *How could I ever have wanted to be him?* I thought in disbelief. But then I got a grip on myself. I had to become Meltdown Man one more time, or Kevin would never leave this place. And neither would I.

I sat down in front of the computer. I touched my fingers to the keyboard. My hands were trembling, and I fought to steady them.

"Go on. Play the game!" Split-Face commanded.

I took a deep breath. I was a good player—maybe the best. But for all the times I'd played the game, I'd never even come close to getting away with Dirk Zorsan's secret formula. He had always beaten me. Then again, it had never been a matter of life and death, like it was now.

I punched the Enter key to begin the game. When the list of players popped up onto the screen, I hesitated for a minute, then chose Meltdown Man.

In a flash the screen filled with a picture of Zorsan's grim fortress. I leaned forward. For a moment I felt dizzy. Then the room around me wavered, faded. I closed my eyes to steady myself.

A minute later, I opened my eyes and gasped. I was in the game.

I *was* Meltdown Man!

Chapter 21

I looked around Meltdown Man's strange cyber world, trying to get my bearings. The minefield was in front of me, and Dirk Zorsan's steel fortress loomed beyond. I formed a quick plan of attack and began to run.

I tore across the minefield and headed for the moat that surrounded the fortress. *Zazoom! Bam!* I dodged from side to side as mines exploded around me. I could feel the searing heat from their terrible fires as I rushed past. I'd made it!

A crocodile darted out of the moat with astonishing speed. His huge jaws were opened, and he was heading for me. I could hear another one climbing out of the water behind the first. *Zap!* I karate-kicked one and then leaped onto the back of the second. He opened his mouth wider. I fixed him in my glance and unleashed the power of my laser vision. Seconds later, he exploded.

I dove into the dark, icy water and climbed up a small hill on the other side of the moat. I had reached the fortress door. A troop of Dirk Zorsan's robots was there to meet me.

Pow! Crunch! Thud! I drop-kicked one and went

hand-to-hand with another. We had moved into the entrance to the fortress now. Our blows thudded against the steel walls.

More robots were coming. I fired up my laser vision again, but I could feel that my power was waning. I was getting tired. It was time for some evasive action.

I ducked through a small door and ran down a long, winding hallway that came out into a large room. Sinister pictures of Dirk Zorsan and his robots lined the dull gray walls. This was Zorsan's picture gallery, the room just above his laboratory. Somewhere in the room was a trapdoor that led straight down into the lab.

I had to find it and steal the secret formula.

Finding it wouldn't be easy, because there were lots of other doors in that room—doors that led only to dungeons or death.

The back of my neck prickled. I fired up my laser vision again, preparing for the fight ahead, but it was still weak. I was well below my full strength, and I could hear Dirk Zorsan's robot troops approaching fast. If I didn't find that door in the next five seconds, I'd be trapped in the game forever.

I looked around the vast room in terror. Then I noticed that one of the pictures hanging on the wall was of someone I knew: Scott Grady.

What was his picture doing in Dirk Zorsan's fortress? Suddenly the picture moved—just slightly.

I caught my breath. The picture was alive.

"Scott?" I said.

He turned his gaze on me, his eyes wide and scared. Then he shook his head. "Forget it," he mouthed at me. "You can't win."

Scott must have played the game for Split-Face. But Scott must have lost!

I whirled away from the picture.

Zorsan's robots were just outside the room. In desperation, I fired up my laser vision and focused it on the steel door. The first robot came through. The laser stopped him, but he didn't melt. He just froze for an instant and then kept coming.

Then I heard laughter behind me. I turned around to see Dirk Zorsan's black hooded figure looming over me. He raised his gun and aimed it in my direction.

Chapter 22

Was this what Scott meant?

You can't win.

I fixed my eyes on Zorsan, rage surging through me. The gun melted in his hand. Yet Zorsan himself just kept coming closer and closer.

What did Scott mean? *Forget it. You can't win.*

Did he mean that it was impossible to win? That even if I stole the secret formula, Split-Face wouldn't let Kevin go and I'd be stuck in this game forever?

I lunged forward as Dirk Zorsan flung himself at me, his razored gloves slicing through the air. I clawed at his face, and then I gasped.

His mask had come off. But the face behind it was the last face I'd expected to see.

"Mr. Allen?" I cried.

Mr. Allen just smiled, his hands reaching out for me.

I hesitated, then sprang forward to fight. But the face in front of me wasn't Mr. Allen's anymore. It had morphed into Corey Wilson's.

"Go on," Corey whispered. "You want your revenge. Take it."

He leered at me mockingly. Then his face twisted into another face I knew: Ted Stern's.

Suddenly it changed yet again. Now, Chris Johnson was staring down at me. "So, you ready to fight, Harper?" he scoffed.

Then I was looking up at Mr. Allen once more. "Show some hustle, Harper," he sneered.

My mind was racing. Who was I fighting anyway? Was I just trying to get revenge on everyone who had ever made fun of me? Was Dirk Zorsan my enemy? Or was it me, Meltdown, who was the real villain here?

Revenge—that was the whole purpose of the game. Split-Face had told me that. That's why I felt so good when I played. No one could beat me—not even all those people who made fun of me.

"What are you waiting for?" Mr. Allen said mockingly. "Don't you want to get me—Fumble-Fingers?"

"No!" I shouted.

Then I blinked. Mr. Allen was gone. There was only the hooded figure of Dirk Zorsan in front of me. His eyes gleamed behind his black mask. He took a step forward. In a moment, he was going to be all over me.

He was going to destroy me.

There was no escape. The game would soon be over, and I was going to lose, unless I fought back.

I glanced over at Scott Grady's portrait. The boy shook his head as if to tell me it was hopeless.

Then, beside the portrait, I saw something: a glimmer of light. I narrowed my eyes. It was a mirror!

In it I could see Meltdown's face. Split-Face's face. *My* face—one side normal, the other hideously scarred.

I drew in my breath as a plan formed in my head. Maybe there was a way to beat Dirk Zorsan. But would I live to see if it worked?

Chapter 23

I fired up Meltdown's laser vision. Then I focused my eyes at the mirror. The brilliant laser light shot out, then bent itself back, striking Meltdown—and me—between the eyes.

For a moment I felt a searing pain all over me. Then nothing.

I blinked. I was sitting in Split-Face's house, leaning over the computer keyboard. Although I could barely catch my breath, I had never been happier. I had destroyed Meltdown Man and made it back alive.

The computer let out a loud, angry beep that sounded like a car alarm. Then letters appeared on the screen. *System error! System error! Abort game? Yes. No.*

"What have you done?" Split-Face shrieked behind me.

Ignoring him, I pressed down *Y* for *Yes.*

The words *game aborted* appeared in the right-hand corner of the screen. Dirk Zorsan's fortress melted before my eyes. But as the cold metal walls disappeared, I saw something that made me happy.

It was the portrait of Scott Grady.

He no longer looked scared and sad.

Scott Grady was smiling.

At that instant, his picture vanished. The screen went black. Then random numbers, letters, and symbols danced across it, looking like spilled alphabet soup.

I had seen a computer screen that looked like that once in Mr. Cochran's class when some new software had malfunctioned. I knew what it meant.

The system had totally crashed.

I lifted my head.

Split-Face was staring at the screen. Then he let out a bloodcurdling howl.

Chapter 24

"**W**hat did you do to the game?" Split-Face screamed. Pushing me aside, he frantically punched codes into the keyboard, but the screen had frozen. Nothing moved.

Split-Face turned to face me. He looked angry enough to kill. "Why did you destroy my game?" he snarled. His blood-red eyes bored into mine. They were crazy eyes, wild with fury. He stretched out his huge arms to grab me.

I scrambled backward.

"Don't hurt him!" Kevin shouted. "It's over. You can't win."

Split-Face peered up at him. The crazy gleam faded from his eyes. He dropped his hands to his sides and sighed.

"It had to happen sometime," he said sadly. "The game couldn't go on. I knew that, but . . ."

"But what?" Kevin prompted gently.

Split-Face pounded his fists on the computer desk. His mouth was twitching with rage. "I wanted revenge!" he howled. "They ruined my life! The horrible people of this town took my life away." His scarred face looked bitter and sad.

Split-Face sank into a chair and buried his face in his hands. He was silent for a moment. Then he looked up and stared blankly ahead as he spoke. "You see, my grandfather, Martin Fury, raised me in this house after my parents died. He was a magician, but not a very good one," he continued, his voice becoming softer.

Then he sneered. "The people in this town thought he was a joke. They laughed at him when he walked down the street. The neighborhood children threw eggs at our house and teased me in school."

Split-Face's eyes shone like flames out of his scarred and twisted face. "So Grandpa decided to show them. He studied black magic and learned to harness the darkest powers of the universe. He was going to teach the whole town just how powerful real magic could be. But one of his final experiments backfired. His studio caught fire, and no one came to help. I tried to save him, but it was too late. He died in the flames."

Split-Face gestured at the ruined skin on his face. "As you can see," he went on sarcastically, "I escaped with my life. I spent the rest of my youth in an orphanage, but I was never happy. No one wanted to be around a monster like me.

"When I grew up, I went to college and studied computers. I learned to program games. I became rich and came back to this house. I planned to use my grandfather's power to make a game that would be my revenge on this town and the people who live here. I studied his journals and became more powerful than he had ever imagined was possible.

"And then I created *The Furious Four*. Using the spells my grandfather taught me and those I'd learned, I invented new magic and mixed it into the game. I designed the game so that anyone playing it who had reason to be as angry as I was would be sucked into my world. They would turn into me—into Meltdown Man. They would have new powers, dark powers they could use to get revenge on everyone who had wronged them. And by getting their revenge, they would help me get mine. Then I put the game on the Internet, but I put a block on it so that only kids from Greenvale would be able to play."

Split-Face let out a spine-chilling laugh.

My eyes widened. So I'd been right. The reason I had loved the game—and Meltdown Man—so much was because I secretly wanted to get revenge on everyone who made fun of me. I swallowed, feeling ashamed.

"But what about now?" I said.

Split-Face turned and glared at me. "You destroyed Meltdown," he said angrily. "You used the magic against him. The game wasn't programmed for that! Meltdown Man lived only for revenge! The game is over."

He rubbed his hands over his face. "Maybe it's for the best," he added quietly. "Maybe it was too late to get revenge. Being angry at people won't bring my grandfather back. And I'll never be rid of these ugly scars."

Once again, I almost felt sorry for Split-Face. But suddenly I remembered Scott Grady and Mr. Allen.

Now that the game was destroyed, what would happen to them? Would they ever come back? I couldn't help feeling scared. Then I thought of something that made me feel better.

Scott Grady had smiled.

He wouldn't have smiled like that if he were doomed to be stuck in the game forever. Would he?

"Is the game really destroyed?" I asked aloud.

"I told you, it's gone."

"But didn't you make any backup discs?" asked Kevin.

I was amazed my friend could think clearly enough to remember discs at a time like this. But Kevin was right. The game had been destroyed on-line, but it could easily be transferred onto the Internet again if there were any copies of it anywhere.

Split-Face nodded. "Yes," he replied. "There is one." He picked up a dark blue disc from the computer desk and turned it over and over in his hands. Then he turned to Kevin and me. His eyes were fiery pools of anger.

"You want to destroy this, too, don't you?" he snarled.

I froze, almost afraid to breathe. Would Split-Face give us the disc?

"Yes," Kevin said firmly. "We do."

Split-Face stood up and towered over Kevin for a moment. Then his shoulders slumped. "It had to happen," he declared tonelessly. "The game had to end. I always knew the game would have to stop sometime."

He thrust the disc into my hand and pushed me

hard. "Take it!" he shouted. "Take it and leave, and don't come back."

Kevin and I didn't hesitate. We turned and ran out of the house. We kept running until we were back at school.

Chapter 25

We dashed breathlessly through the school doors. I glanced up at the clock. It was one-thirty. I found it hard to believe that only two hours had passed since I'd left the building. It felt like a lifetime!

Kevin and I started down the hall. But we didn't get far before our school principal, Mr. Boston, stepped out of his office and blocked our way.

"Kevin Tyler, Matt Harper!" he barked. "Where have you two been? First Mr. Allen disappears. Then you two decide to cut class."

Without even giving us a chance to answer, the principal grabbed me by the arm. "I'll deal with you later, Mr. Tyler," he said. "Matt, you're coming with me to my office. The police want to talk to you immediately!"

"Would you mind taking off your sunglasses?" the police officer asked sternly. I nodded. I'd forgotten I even had them on. With shaking fingers, I removed them.

I blinked. Then I smiled slightly.

My eyes weren't stinging! They felt fine.

Then I looked up and stopped smiling. The police officer was frowning at me. So was Mr. Boston.

The principal cleared his throat. "Matt, Officer Stein here wants to ask you about a very serious matter."

Officer Stein nodded. "I assume you know that your gym teacher, Mr. Allen, has disappeared. We understand that you were the last person to talk to him. A number of witnesses have told us that you two were having a heated argument. Is there anything you can tell us, Matt?"

"Yes, tell us, Matt," cut in Mr. Boston. "Where have you been for the last two hours?"

"I . . ." I faltered. How could I tell them the truth? They'd think I was crazy for sure.

"Go on, Matt," Mr. Boston urged me.

Then the door swung open behind me. Mrs. Willis came rushing in. With her was Mr. Allen.

"We just found Mr. Allen," Mrs. Willis said excitedly. "He was standing in the middle of the playing field." She beamed at Mr. Allen. "Isn't that right?"

Mr. Allen nodded slowly. He looked confused. I couldn't blame him. The last time I'd seen him, he'd been dressed up as the archvillain Dirk Zorsan!

"Mr. Allen, thank goodness you're safe," Mr. Boston exclaimed.

Officer Stein stood up. "Mr. Allen, if you could just tell me your whereabouts for the last two hours . . ."

Mr. Allen blinked. "I don't remember," he said. "It's the strangest thing, but I just can't remember."

Mrs. Willis looked at him with concern. "Maybe he has sunstroke or something," she murmured in an undertone to Mr. Boston.

Mr. Boston and Officer Stein decided to take Mr. Allen to the hospital immediately to make sure there was nothing wrong with him.

"I'm pretty sure I'm fine, though," Mr. Allen said as he was helped out of Mr. Boston's office. "In fact, I never felt better."

I waited for Mr. Boston to turn around and expel me or something. But no one came back. It looked like everyone had completely forgotten about me.

For a moment I just sat in the chair in front of Mr. Boston's big desk. Then waves of relief rolled over me. If Mr. Allen had come back unhurt, there was a good chance—an excellent chance—that Scott Grady was okay, too. Maybe everything really was back to normal.

I wasn't Meltdown Man anymore. There was no more *Furious Four*. The game was destroyed.

For a moment, that made me feel a tiny bit sad. But then I shook myself. Was I crazy? I'd had the powers of a superhero for one day, and I hadn't liked it one bit. I knew I should be grateful that my boring life was back to normal.

The rest of the day was pretty hectic. Mr. Boston didn't go to the hospital with Mr. Allen after all. He walked my gym teacher to the police squad car and then came back into the building. I was walking out of his office when he cornered me.

"You and I still have a little matter to discuss, Mr. Harper," he said sternly. "Have a seat while I ask Mr. Tyler to join us."

I got a three-day suspension and two weeks' detention for cutting class and leaving the school grounds without permission. So did Kevin. Both our moms came to school right away to pick us up. Boy, were they ever mad!

"What in the world's gotten into you, Matt Harper?" Mom raged as we drove home. "You've been acting very oddly lately. Is something going on that your father and I should know about? We're both very concerned."

Then she told me I was grounded for two weeks and that I couldn't touch my computer for at least a week.

That was fine with me, but I didn't tell her that.

I wasn't allowed to watch television, either. But I listened to the news that night through my parents' bedroom door. There were two stories that interested me.

The first was that Scott Grady had turned up. His mother told reporters Scott had just showed up at their house at one-thirty that afternoon. He seemed fine, but his parents had had him checked into a hospital for observation.

Reporters said Scott Grady couldn't remember anything about where he'd been for the last few days. A doctor from the hospital said that people sometimes forgot bad things that they experienced. The doctor went on to say that Scott might never remember what had happened while he was missing.

The second news story was about a mysterious fire on North Adams Street. The gray house had burned to the ground. But neighbors had seen the owner—a Mr. Fury—leaving with a suitcase two hours before the blaze. Police were searching for Mr. Fury, but so far he appeared to have vanished without a trace. The fire chief said that the fire was "suspicious."

That night, before bed, I took the disc containing the last copy of *The Furious Four* out of my backpack. I wanted to destroy it, but I didn't dare get on the computer. If I did, Mom would probably ground me for life!

I placed the disc on my desk, next to my printer. Just one more week, I told myself. Then Meltdown Man is history.

Chapter 26

A week had passed since Kevin and I had escaped from Split-Face's house. Life had gone back to normal—sort of.

The first day of my suspension, Mom found Sherri, Crystal's doll, in the hall closet.

The doll's face was perfect.

"You must think you're pretty clever pulling a stunt like that, Matt," Mom said, shaking her head. "How did you do it? Was it some kind of magic trick?"

I didn't say anything.

"Well, Crystal will be happy when she gets home from school. I think you should give this to her." Mom handed me the doll and walked into the kitchen. I stared into Sherri's glassy blue eyes. They looked brand-new.

Mom was right. Crystal was so excited when I gave her Sherri that she tried to kiss me. I backed away and ran up the stairs and hid out in my room until dinnertime.

"Maybe Matt's planning on being a magician when he grows up," Dad said at dinner that night. "Good magicians never give away their tricks."

He winked at me. "Is that what this is all about, Matt?" Dad joked. "Are you planning a career in magic?"

"No way!" I grimaced. I couldn't tell my parents how close I'd been to being a victim of a magic trick myself. I didn't even like to think about it.

Kevin and I could barely bring ourselves to talk about what had happened that day at Split-Face's house. It all seemed like some crazy nightmare.

I thought a lot about Split-Face, though. Now that I wasn't so scared of him, I truly did feel sorry for him. If I was teased so much just for being short and bad at sports, I could imagine how awful it must have been for Split-Face. His face was so scarred and gruesome. And he had no family to turn to when kids picked on him.

No wonder he wanted revenge.

And I had to admit that the game Split-Face invented *had* been awesome.

Sometimes I almost wished I could play it again. But I knew better. I planned to destroy the disc the moment Mom let me back on my computer.

Then I saw Scott Grady. It happened the day my suspension ended. Mom picked me up from school. On the way home we stopped to pick up a pizza for dinner. I guess she was feeling sorry for me, because she ordered ham and pineapple toppings.

"That's my favorite kind of pizza, too," a voice next to me said. I turned to see who had such good taste, and then I saw him: Scott Grady! He looked a ton better than he had the last time I'd seen him—on Dirk Zorsan's wall. He wasn't wearing dark glasses, for one thing. For another, he wasn't as pale. He definitely didn't look like a ghost anymore.

I stared at him, and he stared at me.

I wondered if what they'd said on the news was true—did he really not remember anything about what had happened after he disappeared? But then he grinned and mouthed two words at me.

It took me a minute to understand what they were. But then I smiled.

Scott Grady had said, "Thanks, partner."

It had been good to have a break from the computer, but I was happy when Mom said I could use it again. Even though I was still grounded, she said she didn't mind if I invited a couple of friends over.

I called up Kevin right away. "Want to come over and fool around on the Net with me?" I asked. His mom had only grounded him for four days.

"Sure," Kevin answered. "I'll be right over!"

When he showed up, Chris was with him. Kevin whispered that Chris had come over just as he was about to set out for my house. He hoped I didn't mind that he'd brought Chris along.

I tried not to mind, but I did.

Chris was in a great mood, though, joking and laughing. In fact, by the time the afternoon was over, I'd almost decided Chris was okay—almost!

The only awkward moment was when Chris wanted to play *The Furious Four*. He searched for it on the Internet directory for over five minutes.

"Wow! How bizarre," he exclaimed. "The game's gone!"

Kevin and I exchanged a glance.

"Yeah, I noticed that yesterday," Kevin said. "But there are lots of other cool MUDs. Why don't we try this one—*Dragon World*?"

"Okay, I guess." Chris sounded disappointed. "But I can't understand why the game would just disappear like that!"

"Me, either," I said. My eyes slid over to the blue disc on the side of my computer. I hadn't erased it yet, but later that night I was going to.

After Kevin and Chris left, I put the disc into my machine. I tried to call up the files so I could delete them, but there were none. The disc was totally blank.

Split-Face must have made a mistake, I thought. *The backup disc was probably destroyed when the house burned down.*

At least, that was what I believed until the next morning.

I had just finished my yucky oatmeal—it wasn't so bad if you put a ton of maple syrup on it—when I heard Mom calling to me. "Matt! Kevin and Chris are here to walk you to school."

I ran to the door. "Hey, Matt," Kevin greeted me. His voice sounded funny.

"Hey, Kevin," I said. Then my eyes slid over to Chris.

"Hi, Chris," I mumbled. This time my voice sounded funny, too. Chris was wearing a pair of sunglasses.

Big, black sunglasses.

I stood there for a long moment, thinking about the disc that Split-Face had given me. Chris couldn't have stolen the disc on my desk and replaced it with another one, could he?

"So, Chris, what's with the new look?" I asked nervously.

Chris smirked at me. "You mean my shades? I don't know. I guess I must have allergies or something. When I woke up this morning, my eyes were stinging."

Then Chris lifted his sunglasses. His eyes looked red—very red. My heart started thumping.

"Those allergies must be bad," I said slowly.

"The worst." Chris smirked again. Then he turned and looked at the huge plotted plant my Mom kept on our porch. It was a big pink geranium.

The flowers began to shrivel and turn brown, letting off a little ribbon of smoke. In a few moments, the plant was a withered husk. Chris lowered the glasses back over his eyes.

I gulped.

"So, you ready to go, Matt?" Chris said with a toothy grin.

"Are you sure you're okay?" I asked cautiously. "Allergies can make you feel pretty bad."

"Not me," Chris said, peering over the top of his sunglasses. "I feel just great!"

VISIT PLANET TROLL

A super-sensational spot on the Internet
at http://www.troll.com

Check out Kids' T-Zone, a really cool place where you can...

- Play games!
- Win prizes!
- Speak your mind in the Gab Lab!
- Find out about the latest and greatest books and authors!
- Shop at BookWorld!
- Order books on-line!

And a UNIVERSE more of GREAT BIG FUN!

Don't miss the next exciting

Lost in Dino World

by S. F. Black

Brooke is thrilled to find a new friend on the Internet. He goes by the name "Lizard Boy," and he seems to know more about dinosaurs than anyone she's ever met. But when Brooke enters the Dino World chat room, she has a chance to meet the mysterious Lizard Boy at last. And now she's in for the surprise—and fright—of her life.

0-8167-4280-4